# WATER STEPS

Also by A. LaFaye

# WATER STEPS

A. LaFaye

milkweed
editions

© 2009, Text by A. LaFaye

Published 2009 by Milkweed Editions
Printed in Canada
Cover design by Kristine Mudd
Cover photo: Sam Diephuls, Getty Images
Author photo by Rhonda Hunt
Interior design by Steve Foley
The text of this book is set in ITC Giovanni Book.
09 10 11 12 13   5 4 3 2 1
*First Edition*

Please turn to the back of this book for a list of the sustaining funders of Milkweed Editions.

Library of Congress Cataloging-in-Publication Data

LaFaye, A.
  Water steps / A. LaFaye.—1st ed.
        p. cm.
  Summary: Eleven-year-old Kyna has been terrified of water since a storm drowned her family and nearly took her as well, but works to overcome her phobia when her adoptive parents, Irish immigrants with a mysterious past, rent a cabin on Lake Champlain for the summer.
  ISBN 978-1-57131-686-8 (pbk. : alk. paper)—ISBN 978-1-57131-687-5 (cloth : alk. paper)
[1. Phobias—Fiction. 2. Water—Fiction. 3. Irish Americans—Fiction. 4. Silkies—Fiction. 5. Orphans—Fiction. 6. Champlain, Lake—Fiction.] I. Title.
  PZ7.L1413Wat 2009
  [Fic]—dc22
                    2008011684

To every kid who faces a fear
and finds a little magic

# WATER STEPS

*Thanks to everyone at Milkweed Editions for bringing this book out into the world, to my students at Plattsburgh State University who shared the magic of the lake, and to God for providing the inspiration for this novel.*

# WATER STEPS

# AIR

Any old dummy can take a digital photograph.
But how many kids can take a real old-fashioned
shutter shot of a purple hairstreak butterfly in flight?
Not too many. That's how I earned a red ribbon at the
Cortland County Fair last year. I could've taken the
first place blue if it weren't for Gaylen Parker, the girl
with gigabytes for brains.

She had to enter with her digitally muckety-
mucked picture of a Pocono Mountains sunset. No
way does nature paint with that kind of a brush, but
computers sure do. She can swear to fifty thousand
judges that she didn't fix-up that photograph, but
I'm not going to buy it. Thanks to her cheating,

pixel tweaking pinkies, I lost the blue.

"Too bad you can't get her to spit in water, Kyna," Pep told me the morning after the fair. He's always coming up with these wacky Irish traditions no one but the leprechauns have heard of.

"What good would that do?" I asked, helping him set the table for breakfast.

He paused, cocked his eyebrows, then said, "Well, some folks say if a liar spits in water it doesn't float."

"Did you pick that up from one of your fairy friends?" I asked. I needed a real solution to my problem, not fairy dust.

"How many times do I have tell you? Fairies aren't friendly. They're pony-riding, baby-stealing little fiends, those fairies."

Pep always spoke of the make-believe critters from his Irish homeland as if they were as everyday as the village priest. A running joke he'd played with Mem since the day they adopted me. I tried to tell them I was too old for all their shenanigans, but Pep just told me they'd have to be leprechauns to get up to any, so that was that.

Coming in from the garden with some nasturtium greens for the salad, Mem said, "All that Parker girl would have to do is eat a bit of salt before she spits,

Ronan. You should know the way around that test better than anyone." Dumping the greens into the bowl next to Pep, she elbowed him, saying, "Mr. *'I've got tickets to see the Chieftains in Dublin.'*"

"I had them. Just couldn't use them. A bit damp they were."

They laughed. I'd heard the story of the soggy concert tickets he found on a rock along the shore a thousand times, how he used the promise of them to get Mem to finally go out with him, then hid them until they'd reached a pretty cove south of Dublin for a moonlit swim. I knew that story word for word, but I still loved the way it made them laugh, then start chattering in Irish, their hands flashing to the rhythm of the memories they told each other.

They'd smile, fall shoulder to shoulder, then finally remember I was still standing there and one of them would say, "Sorry, sweet, little swim down the memory channel, there."

No matter. I'd taken a little trip down memory lane, myself. I prefer land travel. I went back to the day I finally got my shot of the purple hairstreak. I'd been hanging out in the Garrington Gardens on Clark Street for days. My kind of place. In the center of the town of Perryville, high in the Pocono

Mountains of Pennsylvania, plenty far from the ocean. The park didn't even have a pond. I spent my days there hovering over flowers, my camera focused and ready for just the right bug to fly into view. I had shot after shot of bees and moths, and I almost caught a hummingbird beak-deep in a honeysuckle, but I sneezed, so all I got was a big blur of a photograph and a bruised eye from where I clonked into the camera.

But there's something triple-chocolate-cheesecake good about hanging there with my camera ready, the *I'm-going-to-get-it-today* tension of waiting for just the right shot that can't be beat. Not with skateboarding or tree climbing or any of the other kooky kid things my classmates are always going on about. I'll take a camera and a roost on a good rock any day.

And the *gotcha* moment makes it worth the leg-cramping wait. After two weeks at my flower post, I snapped the shot just as the purple hairstreak opened its wings a flutter above a yellow rose and I knew I'd caught a miracle right by the antennae. You couldn't buy that with a zillion dollars or a truckload of blue ribbons.

And I even got my picture in the paper for all of that hard work. Actually, the whole family is in the picture. Me in the middle with my picture held up, Mem and Pep on either side, squeezing me for pride's sake. So what if it was only half the size of Gaylen's and on the fourth page of the family section. This year I'd take a picture no silly computer could touch. They'd pin that pretty blue ribbon on there and we'd have a nice big picture on page one.

That was the plan until Mem and Pep came up to my room in the attic, looking all *"we've got something to tell you and you're not going to like it."* Didn't matter if I had a summer full of plans. Sure, I wanted to get a shot not even Gaylen Parker could beat. But I also had some great ideas for summer upgrades on my tree fort in the backyard and my best friend Hillary and I planned to start our Get With the Land project for Girl Scouts in the state park by mapping all the walking trails complete with nature guide signs along the way. I even saved up my allowance to buy a compass. I had my whole summer set for great adventure, but no, Mem and Pep had other plans that washed all of mine away.

They plopped down at the end of my bed, knee to knee, knuckle to knuckle, as they cranked up the smiles.

"What?" I asked, not wanting to know.

They put on their fake chipper voices, then Mem said, "We have a plan."

Pep must have seen the *bury me now* look on my face, because he said, "An opportunity, really."

"We've rented a cabin for the summer."

No way would they pull me in with their little bait. I'd just wait for the hook. The hard barby piece of the news I couldn't swallow.

"And . . ." Pep couldn't say it. That spelled bad news to me. I gripped the seat of my chair.

Mem leaned forward and whispered, "It's on a lake."

Pep jumped in with, "A magical lake with silkies in it."

A lake?! Felt like they'd sucked all of the air out of my lungs with straws. I couldn't live on a lake. I'd rather be chopped up and fed to lions. Live in the middle of the desert in a tin shed. Spend the summer on a frozen tundra ice floe with a parka and a pick. But not near water. Please, no water.

# WATER

Water scared me. Freaked me out so much I couldn't walk through a rain puddle. My bones locked up. My muscles shrank. I turned to stone. The whole world went blue. Water scared me that much and Mem and Pep wanted me to live by a lake for the summer. A magic lake they said. Filled with silkies—the seal folk who take on human form when they leave the water. I didn't care if the lake itself could fly!

I didn't want to live on a lake. I didn't want to live near a lake. I didn't want to even see a picture of a lake.

Moving from the bed to kneel next to me, Pep said, "You don't have to get in the lake, Kyna. You won't

7

even be able to see the water from the house. It sits high up on the shore. Nice and dry."

"But I'll know the water's there, Pep. I'll hear it," I said, diving on the bed to roll up in my quilt.

Kissing me through the quilt, Mem said, "You can't let your fears grow bigger than you, Kyna. They'll swallow you up."

My fear of water was as big as a lake. And I'd drown in it.

But I knew the rules. Face your fear one step at a time. Speaking through the quilt, I asked, "I don't have to go in the water?"

"Not until you're ready." Mem rubbed my back.

Pep and Mem always said, "Not until you're ready."

They got this great slogan from Dr. Clark, the therapist they dragged me to every week. Worked just fine for me when it came to being ready to sleep over at a friend's house or ride my bike downtown, but sometimes Mem and Pep thought I was ready before I really was. Last fall, they wanted me to take a shower. Not a slimy sponge bath in my nice dry bedroom on the third floor, but a shower in the tub that could fill up with water.

I refused and locked myself in my closet, yelling, "If you make me take a shower, I'll never bathe again."

Speaking through the door, Mem said, "Then you'll smell so bad animals will roll on you for the scent."

Our cat, Kippers, loved to roll on dirty socks and stick her head in my smelly shoes. I imagined myself walking outside, attracting every cat in the neighborhood. They'd rub all over me until I fell into the grass and disappeared under a pile of purring fur.

But the closet felt too small and dark. I had to open the door.

Pep gave me a hug and a kiss on the forehead.

"We'll be right there with you, Kyna," he said, already in his swim trunks—the green ones with the dancing sea horses. He has as many swimming trunks as he does pants. But he calls them *togs*.

"Can I bring my snorkle?" I held it up. Some kids have a security blanket. I have a breathing device for anything I have to do with water.

"No." Mem shook her head. She wore the silver swimsuit that sparkled in the sun like the scales of a fish.

"But the tub could fill up with water."

"The drain's clear. I checked it just this evening," Pep said, coming to my other side.

"It could clog up with hair and soap while we're in there."

"We won't let it." Mem gave me a big squeeze. "Come on, you'll see."

They led me into the hall.

I dragged my feet, shouting, "I'm not ready!"

"Yes, you are," Mem said, as she swept my legs out from under me and carried me down the two flights of stairs to the bathroom. The room I hated most of all. The room I enjoyed having two full stories below me because it had water—everywhere. The sink. The toilet. The tub.

How did she know I was ready? Didn't she hear me gasping for breath? Feel the cold sweat on my palms? The tight grip I had around her neck? As soon as she set me down and I felt the cool tiles under my feet, my body turned as stiff as those tiles.

Pep got in the shower. "I'll show you." I closed my eyes as he turned on the water. "Look at me, Kyna."

I squeezed my eyes tight, so I didn't have to see the water running over his face, near his mouth and nose, crowding up the spaces where breathing air is supposed to go.

Mem hugged me from behind and gave me a nudge with her knees. "Look, Kyna."

Pep stood in the tub, the water washing over his shoulders, not his face. "See, just a little wetness. A little cool cleanness." He rubbed the water over his skin.

"Let's try it," Mem said, stepping forward, bumping me ahead of her.

"Just my hand!" I screamed, putting it out.

"First your hand," Mem said.

Shaking, I closed my eyes and put my hand forward, felt the tiny *pat pat* of the water. Rain. Rain leads to storms. Storms drown people at sea! I yanked my hand away and buried my face in Mem's tummy. I'll take hand sanitizer any day. Thank you very much.

"Try again, Kyna," Pep said. "Just think of it as a little wash up in a very big sink."

Sink? Huh! No one's ever drowned in a sink.

Rubbing my back, Mem turned me around, then said, "Go on, both hands this time around. Then one foot. Little water steps."

Water steps. We'd been taking water steps ever since we started visiting Dr. Clark. And sometimes, just sometimes, it made me wish they'd never adopted me.

Mem made me take my first water step when she put a tiny pool of water on the back of my hand and wouldn't let me wipe it off. I was only three years old, but I felt sure it would spread and spread until it drowned me. But Mem did it again the next day, then the next and the next until I could look straight at that water touching my skin and not panic.

That spring, I had to put my whole hand in a bowl of water. When the water slipped over my skin, I felt sure it could pull me in. Had me gasping for breath in seconds. The leaves started to fall from the trees before I could do it without panting.

The summer before I started school, Mem began to put a glass of water on the table at every meal. Seeing that water just sitting in that glass still as you please set my stomach to sailing on rough seas. That first night, she set it on the far corner, then inched it closer to me each day. Bit by bit, the storm in my stomach lost its steam. When the glass got near enough for me to see the bubbles inside, I had to close my eyes, but I kept the sea calm in my stomach.

One month we worked on me holding the glass until I could stop shaking, then I had to put my lips on the rim. By the time pre-school started, I could take a sip of water without gagging.

In kindergarten, I graduated to wet wash cloth wipe downs. Now I can take a short shower if I keep the door open, but that's not enough for Mem and Pep. They want me to take the next step and live on a lake for a summer. A whole summer. I'd never sleep.

As soon as I close my eyes, I'd see myself drowning.

Drowning is my first memory.

*Water choking me as it filled my nose and mouth, flooding my lungs. I kicked. I coughed. I spun, but I only sank deeper. My whole body aching, the world disappearing into darkness as I sank.*

*I remember smooth arms cradling me, the whooshing rush of water pressing against me as we sped to the surface, but the darkness took me before we broke into the night air.* To this day, I ache to remember that first breath.

As Mem tells it, she and Pep hid in a cave on the seashore to wait out a terrible storm. The sea had grown angry while they swam by the shore. It whipped and churned like a sheet held in the hands of many frenzied children, snapping it up and down from all sides. The ships at sea were tossed like so many balls thrown on the sheet—my family's boat among them.

The folks around town say my father had been a good seaman who even sailed the treacherous waters of Tierra del Fuego down on the tip of South America—a patch of sea so fierce it'd been sinking boats for hundreds, maybe even thousands of years. Seaman or no seaman, he couldn't navigate that terrible storm off the coast of Maine. The sea had gone to war with the wind. Our boat got caught up in the battle. They tugged and pulled at the boat. The wind pushed it toward the shore. The sea bashed it into the rocks.

Mem and Pep stood in the cave, holding each other, praying the boat would survive. But it began to sink. Rushing down the rocks, Mem and Pep dove into the angry sea to rescue my family. They could only save me. The sea swallowed my whole family. My mother, who had wax white skin and red hair. My father, who had a gap in his mustache, right below his nose. My brother, Kenny, who wore a berry blue coat when he went to sea. And even my Grandma Bella, who wore a yellow rubber hat like the deep-sea fisherman you see on the package of fish sticks.

I hate fish sticks, but I love the box. It makes me think of Grandma Bella. I don't remember her. I can't. I was just a toddle-about baby when that boat sank. I only know my family from the pictures—all the pictures that Mem and Pep put in frames for me and spread throughout that narrow little house on Larpin Street in Perryville that'd belonged to Grandma Bella.

Mem and Pep did everything they could to keep me close to my family—fight for the house our family lived in with Grandma Bella, use all the furniture my family had lived with before the sea took them, and hang every last picture of my family they could find. My family was at sea in so many of those pictures, their faces wide with smiles, the sun forcing them to squint. They loved the sea. I hate it.

And no matter how many water steps Mem and Pep force me to take, I'll still hate the sea. Now. Forever. And always. I won't go live on a lake for the summer. I won't.

# LAKE

Mem and Pep had it all rigged. They'd had it rigged for months. I tried to tell them I had to stay home if I ever hoped to take a picture that would earn me a blue ribbon at the Cortland County Fair.

But they had a defense for that one. "They have a Clinton County Fair in Plattsburgh, New York, not twenty minutes from our lake house," Pep told me.

Mem sweetened the pot with, "We'll even take you to New York City for some great shots in Central Park, if you're up for it."

But I didn't really even hear her because I couldn't get over Pep calling it "*our* lake house," like we owned it and it wasn't just a place we rented for the summer.

To make things even worse, they rented our cute little house in Perryville to a family with two hairy, smashed-faced dogs that grunted when they ran. I couldn't stay behind unless I wanted to defend Kippers against grunting dust mops all summer.

Then Hillary told me her parents wanted her to go stay with her grandmother for a month while they taught a class in Mexico. Grandma Homzie lived in a one-bedroom apartment. Hillary slept on the couch. There'd be no room for me.

And no matter how hard I searched, I couldn't find a summer camp that didn't include swimming. Even the Ven Valley Horse Camp had swimming lessons—with your horse!

I had to go live on a lake. A huge, enormous, pool of drowning water.

As we drove to the stupid lake, I tried to draw a map of the one trail Hillary and I had cleared and marked with the posts we'd made ourselves, but Mem and Pep kept telling me silly silkie tales.

They dropped folktales into a conversation like other parents told *when-I-was-your-age* stories. But Mem and Pep's were no Cinderella-type tales. And even though I'd heard them enough to recite them backward, I still listened because I always hoped Mem and Pep might let something about themselves slip. Other kids heard about the time their parents got caught taking a neighbor's bike for a spin or trying to sneak into an R-rated movie, but the only things I knew about my parents were that Pep tricked Mem into dating him with soggy Chieftains tickets and that they decided to honeymoon in the U.S. because they'd heard about the fabulous beaches, ferries, and islands off the coast of Maine. That vacation had become a permanent move to the U.S. when they adopted me.

But if they missed home, they never showed it by telling me tales of their childhood. No, I had to hear about a goofy mythical creature who could've used a map. Silkie lore. No stories about those lifeguardy creatures would make me feel safer about being near that lake.

"They guide ships through dark waters," Mem said, her eyes squinting as if she led a ship herself.

"I won't be on a ship in any waters," I said, petting Kippers.

Pep tapped the steering wheel. "Now Kyna, if you're swimming . . ."

"Swimming!" I sat forward. "I'm never going swimming."

"Just listen, love." He smiled into the rearview

19

mirror at me. "If a swimmer, any swimmer, were to have a bit of trouble in a silkie lake, the silkies would rescue them. You can't drown in a silkie lake."

"Pft!" I crossed my arms. "What's a silkie doing in an American lake anyway?"

"They're immigrants, like us," Mem said.

Pep lowered his voice into adventure-story mode, then said, "In a summer so warm folks thought the North Pole might melt, a pod of silkies set to sea. Young adventuresome silkies they were. Wild ones who grew up on stories of the seal folk who guided Leif Erikson on his journey over the great ocean. They swam clear to Canada, right into the Gulf of St. Lawrence. Slipping into the St. Lawrence River, most of the pod made their way to the Great Lakes for a bit of a holiday.

"But as the story goes, a young silkie lad named Terin got himself turned around. The water had lost its salt and gone murky green long about twilight. His lungs hurt with that weak, salt-free water. And the sounds didn't travel right, bouncing off rocks and the riverbed. With the water all shallow and filled with tiny rushing currents, he got tangled up in a batch of weeds, misheard the calls from the front of the pod, and went the wrong way down the Richelieu

River. Finding him missing, a few of his kinfolk went hunting, winding their way down rivers and streams.

"Meanwhile, Terin came out in Lake Champlain, a grand, beautiful, clear lake filled with islands to the north and reflecting great gray mountains topped with pine trees to the southwest. But aye, what he loved the best were the rolling green hills to the east. What with the rocky shore and the green hills and the mist of the morning, Terin felt himself at home. And when his aunties and uncles found him there, swimming along the shores, they too had to agree with him. And there they stayed.

"That's how the silkies came to Lake Champlain."

"Oh yeah? When did the leprechauns show up?" I asked.

"And how would they do that?" Pep asked. "Have you ever seen a rainbow big enough to cross the Atlantic?" He glanced back at me. "Well, have you?"

"No." I rolled my eyes.

"Well, then, there you have it. They can't get here, now can they?"

"Why not just buy a plane ticket over?"

Mem laughed, "I can see them all standing on each other's shoulders to hand off a wee passport to the customs officer." She squeaked up her voice, "'We're traveling for pleasure, sir. Off to see the rainbows cast by Niagara Falls, sir. See what they've got at the end of them.'"

Mem acted out what she described. "And the big one on the bottom's all red faced and shaking. A minute later, they all tumble to the ground in a screaming pile of buckles and hats, poking out feet and elbows everywhere like some muddled-up hedgehog."

We all laughed.

"And can you imagine trying to buckle a leprechaun into an airplane seat? One good bout of turbulence and he'd go sailing." She zoomed her hand through the air. "Probably end up in some lady's handbag."

All the crazy stories and I almost forgot where we were headed. Then Pep pulled down a long tree-lined road. I could see the tall gray mountains in the distance to the south—craggy like the wrinkled faces of old men with pine tree beards and pointy hats. I feared these were the mountains to the south of Lake Champlain.

"Are we getting close?" I asked, sinking down in my seat.

"Why?" Pep asked. "Are you excited to jump out and see if you can catch sight of a silkie?"

"No. Just planning an escape route."

Mem frowned at me. "And what if this is meant to be your best summer ever? You're ruining any chance of that with your sour thoughts."

Best? Try worst. I'd never sleep. They'd expect me to eat slimy fish. And those mop dogs would probably drool, chew, and piddle their way through my attic bedroom back home. I'd be lucky if I'd even survive my eleventh summer of life. I'd certainly never forget it!

# HOUSE

We came to a gravelly halt in front of a big old house with a stone foundation, wide gray shutters that looked like splintered wood, and large boxy windows in the roof that looked out over the trees like bulging eyes.

Staring at the attic window eyes that faced the lake as I got out of the car, I said, "My bedroom doesn't face the water does it?" I loved my attic bedroom at home, far away from the downstairs bathroom, but I didn't want to be anywhere near a good view of that lake.

"Not at all." Pep said, lugging a suitcase out of the trunk. "Your bedroom's the back one, right there." He pointed to a bay window above the back door.

"Come on, Kippers." I put the cat down, keeping his leash in my hand, and walked him inside. Kippers liked to think of himself as a dog, so he traveled on a leash and played fetch with superballs.

His leash hook jingled and echoed through the nearly empty rooms. I could even hear his claws clickety clacking on the hardwood floors. I didn't like the silence of the place. It made me feel like an invader.

My bedroom had two bay windows. One faced west to look over a small stone courtyard between the driveway and an old stone shed. The other window faced north to a ring of shrubby trees not even big enough to hold a birdhouse, let alone a tree fort like mine. At least I couldn't see the lake. But the echoey bigness of the room made me kind of thin inside.

Even the closet was big enough for a bed. Big old houses with wood floors and echoey rooms had long histories. And histories hid ghosts. I didn't like it one bit. I had half a mind to dig out our tent and sleep outside in the woods to the east. I had my Camping Badge. Why not put it good use? I even started searching the boxes for my tent until I realized camping outside would probably mean I could hear the waves lapping at the shore, threatening to flood. Scratch that plan.

Instead, I left Kippers to roam the house and Mem and Pep to unpack. I headed for the road we came in on, thinking I might find a mountain path I could map out for our Get With the Land project. Besides, heading for high ground sounded like a nice, dry way to spend the summer.

# FIRE

Fire is the enemy of water. Flames can turn drowning waves into steam. I love fire. The quick flash and turn of the flames, the warming heat, and the way it burns the outer edge of marshmallows to a crunchy crust while warming the middles to a creamy mush, just perfect for s'mores. I love fire.

The fireplace in what Mem and Pep called "our lake home" had to be big enough to roast an elephant. So sitting there in front of the rumbling flames on our first night there, I felt safe. I loved the warmth on my tuckered-out toesies, the way the flames made the pine needles stuck in my clothes smell up the room like a tree at Christmas, and the light patterns that flickered over the walls. Even Mem opening the lakeside windows to let out the heat and let in the cool night air didn't touch my cozy mood. And the sweet goo of s'mores made me feel even better.

Then Mem wrapped me up in a bed of knitted blankets by the fire. I nestled down to sleep with the taste of chocolaty marshmallows on my lips, which helped me keep my mind on the sooty logs crumbling, the ashes hissing. But the water started creeping in, lapping and rolling against rocks, raking at my nerves. I closed my eyes against the sound, hoping the crackle and pop of the flames would drown out the ugly sound of waves. But another sound broke in with a squawky kind of rhythm. Was it music from a beach house down the way?

No, it sounded like chirping or an animal kind of chortle. A dolphin? Was Mem playing another "sounds of the sea" CD to get me used to the sound of waves? I sat up to listen.

Nothing but the twittering of a mockingbird starting off its nightly songs in the tree at the corner of the house. Those waves sure played tricks with sound. I burrowed down into my little nest of blankets and focused on the flames, hoping they could keep my mind off the water.

But fires die. And waves go on forever. They washed into my early morning dreams, spilling over the side of the tub in my mind's eye . . . *The shower is on too high. I sputter for air as I struggle to find the knobs to turn the water off. Waves keep crashing in, spraying me with water, pooling at my feet, then my ankles, then my knees. I fumble with the knobs, my hands wet and slippery. I can't get a grip to turn them.*

*When I scream, water fills my mouth, choking me. I can't run. Water surrounds the tub as if it's been set adrift in the sea. I can see the water turning black with the memory of the stormy waves that nearly killed me—churning me into the depths, choking the breath out of me.*

"Kyna! Kyna!" Pep called to me from above like a voice from the clouds.

Turning my head, I could see him, his face wet, his mouth twisted up in fear.

"You're safe, sweet. It's all a dream. Just a dream."

Feeling his legs along my sides, his arms around my chest, hugging me, I felt safe. "The tub was at sea. The shower wouldn't turn off. The waves kept coming in!"

Pep nodded, rubbing my back. "It's all gone now. You're dry and safe here in the living room."

"But you're wet." I reached up and touched his spiky wet hair.

He sniffled. "Sorry, sweet. We went for a morning swim. Shouldn't have left you alone."

I wanted to melt. Mem and Pep loved water more than I loved fire, even more than I loved s'mores. Sometimes, I wondered if they loved it more than me. That's why they made me take water steps. Made me spend the whole summer by a lake. So they could go swimming any time they wanted. My melting feeling turned to flaming anger.

I spun around to get on all fours. "Is that why we're here?" I shoved my blankets aside. "So you can swim? No more scaly skin from too much chlorine. No need to pack up and head to the Y. You can just dive on in!"

Pep held his breath for a second, then folded his arms and legs in front of him. "And what if that were so?"

"You know I hate the water. You know I do!" I shook from the inside.

"And your mem and I love it."

"More than me?" I whispered.

He closed his eyes, then got to his knees in front of me. "Kyna, no man can love a thing as he loves his daughter." He put his hand over my heart. "I just wish you and I could love the same things."

"I won't go swimming with you, Pep. Never."

"*Never*'s an ugly word that closes the mind to wonderful things." He kissed me on the forehead, then stood up. As he headed toward the kitchen, he changed the subject as fast as he switched rooms. "They've got a farmer's market in town. Shall we buy enough vegetables to make the rabbits jealous?"

"And enough fruit to make the monkeys fall from the trees," I added, knowing what he'd say next. Pep was trying to cheer me up. But I felt stuck. Mem and Pep wanted me to change. Become someone else. Someone who could swim. Wasn't plain old me enough?

I heard a door open and close on the lake side of the house. Pep headed in that direction as Mem called out, "The air's full of bees making the flowers spread! Who's up and ready to admire their handiwork?"

Pep spoke, but I couldn't hear him. Mem let out a mournful, "Oh."

I snuck closer to listen in.

# FRUIT

Mem and Pep spoke Irish in quick chirpy bursts like birds fighting over the same feeder. I could've sat in their mouths and still not understood what they said. Mem and Pep wouldn't teach me Irish, asking what half-sane parent would give up a secret language? And I've never found a library or a bookstore with Irish language tapes. So their language stays a secret, just like their past.

When I ask to hear about her Irish childhood, Mem says, "Weren't nothing in my childhood but a bunch of swimming and we all know how you love to hear about swimming." She'll bug out her eyes and blow out her cheeks to make a fish face.

And I laugh. But I still want to know. Did she have brothers and sisters? Live in a little town with cobblestone streets and wandering sheep like you see in the movies?

Once, I asked if they had childhood pictures I could see and Pep said, "Do you like feet? How about sky? Lots of sky? Or maybe you favor bits of mashed up colors? Those are the kinds of pictures my family took. You'd think they'd never touched a camera in their lives."

Mem sputtered out a laugh, saying, "Our family pictures got dropped in a pond."

And when I tried to ask who dropped them or who took those sky-feet pictures, Mem and Pep would change the subject like they always did. Just like that day at the lake house, we went from me wondering who they loved better, me or the water, to plans for a trip to the farmer's market in town.

Mem and Pep did their quick change act, then showed up in shorts and sun hats. "Ready for a trip into town?" Mem asked, setting her hat straight.

A trip to town might not be bad. I could see if they had a good camera store. Might find a new camera bag fit for hiking in the mountains. "How far's this town from the lake then?"

"Oh, a good few feet." Pep squinted in thought.

"Even the town's on the lake?"

"It's a big lake."

Mem added, "Governor of Vermont tried to get it declared a Great Lake," as she herded me out the door.

"Can't we go to the mountains for the day? A good hike to give our lungs a stretch?"

"After you learn the backstroke."

I skidded to a stop in the gravel drive. "Never!"

"Just remember, that's what they said about people learning to fly," Pep said as he opened the car door.

Why did I always get the feeling my parents had learned a thing or two from the Pied Piper about luring children into doing things they didn't want to do?

Not only was Plattsburgh on the lake, but Pep said the farmer's market was only feet from the shore. I waited on the hood of the car and shouted my orders in. "Buy some watermelon! And cherries. Do they have cherries?" Everyone stared at me. But not Mem and Pep. No, they just kept shopping, picking up melons and smelling them like the out-of-towners they were. Who smells fruit?

But I had to admit that the way the lake played with the sun and sent raindrops of light onto the fruit made me wish I could sneak a little closer and take a picture. The drops of light, the bright fruity colors of green, yellow, and red—it'd make a great picture for the fair. Why didn't they get me a zoom lens for Christmas like I'd asked?

"What, and have you tip over?" Pep had teased. "Those things weigh half as much as you do."

Pep had what I called the diversion tactic approach to parenting. First he tried to distract me with his sense of humor. Making me laugh so I didn't realize I'd gotten a knitted jumper (that's Irish for sweater) for Christmas, again. Then he'd try tricky little trades to make me take another water step. If I'd actually washed my hair in the shower by the first of December, he'd have bought me that zoom lens I asked for.

He was a real trickster all right. But he wouldn't trick me into liking that stupid lake. But that didn't keep him from trying. He turned to me with bananas for ears, but I didn't laugh. I wouldn't laugh no matter what kind of fruit he put on his head.

"Taking pictures of the shoppers?" some kid asked me, his hair looking like he used a clam shell to comb it.

"No."

He looked to the market, then to me. "Then why are you sitting over here?"

Thinking of Pep and his feet-sky pictures, I took a snap of the sky. "Better view of the clouds over here."

The kid pulled himself up on the hood of the car like it was nothing more than a neighborhood fence, then said, "The townies treat me like I've got cooties." He hung his head, then sat up real quick, shouting, "But I don't!"

Hey, he didn't have to tell me about feeling like an outsider. The kids in my class think I'm a total camera geek. Not to mention my whole water problem.

He nodded to the camera and pulled me out of my little self-pity party. "You pretty good with that thing?"

"Good enough." I shrugged. Call me kooky, but I get all nervous around other kids in the summer. They always want to go swimming and stuff. If they ask me to go, then they find out I'm nothing but a big sissy. It's like being the only kid at a slumber party who's still afraid of the monsters under the bed.

"Can you take pictures at night with it?" He leaned in to have a look, like he could see if the camera might be able to do such a thing.

"Maybe. But it takes special film." I didn't like the *can-I-borrow-that?* look on his face. Nobody used my camera. It's as important to me as swimming is to Mem and Pep. Like breathing.

I pulled my camera away, but he just leaned back on the hood and changed the subject. "Yeah, I was all excited about having a lake house until I got a load of the beaches here—more rocks than sand. Going barefoot's out. You've got to wear boat shoes. Or should I say, 'rock shoes'?"

He smiled at me to wait for a laugh. When none came, he said, "Was it a long drive for you? We live near Pittsburgh, so it takes a day to get here."

He had that fishing-for-a-friend kind of stubbornness. Maybe if he didn't like the beaches, he wouldn't ask me to go swimming. I decided to see what he had in mind. "We live in a small town called Perryville, near Scranton."

"My grandparents live here. Our lake house is on their land."

I imagined that the boy and his family lived in a cozy cabin by the water and his grandparents lived in a nice big place on the hill among the trees, where they just had to look at the water. They'd have warm log walls and a big fireplace. They'd cuddle together on the couches at night with afghans the grandmother knitted and they'd tell stories by the fire. I'd like to do that myself if we could leave out anything that can fly, guide ships, or grant wishes.

"Can I meet your grandparents?"

"Sure." The boy nodded, his cowlick waving at me. "They're over there picking out veggies for a stew." He pointed to the other end of the market, just feet from the water.

Just the idea of being that close to the lake chilled my bones. I turned away. "Maybe later."

"We're neighbors, you know."

"Really?" Might not be a bad thing, especially if he was keen on hanging out in the woods around our place. I might be able to get some good shots of forest critters, especially if I got some night film—raccoons, possums, maybe even a fox. Or better yet, an owl in flight. We could build a camera post in the trees and I could get an owl spread-wing with its great yellow eyes all aglow. Beat that, Gaylen Parker.

"My grandparents know the owners of your house, the Kenricks. They can't come up to the lake this year because Mrs. Kenrick broke her leg."

That's what I should've done. Jumped from my tree fort and broken my leg. You can't go in the water with a cast. Why didn't I think of that?

"Anyway, they said they rented it to a family with

a kid my age." If the town kids wouldn't play with him, he probably figured he could make friends with another kid on vacation.

We sat there a second, waiting for one of us to say something cool. I thought of asking him what he thought of a nighttime photo shoot, but he said, "Name's Tylo Bishop. When we go back home, I'll be in fourth grade."

"I'll be in fifth. I'm Kyna." Fifth grade meant a trip to the Bighorn Water Park. My school went every year. Maybe just a sprained ankle would get me out of that. I hear there's lots of stairs to climb at those water parks.

"Tylo!" called a woman carrying a watermelon to her car. A trio of boys swarmed her, one of them dive-bombing her with corncob airplanes, another zipping in and out using a plastic wrapped plate of sweets as a steering wheel, and the last one walking kind of crossways, trying to look aloof and cool as he carried a bright pink bag bulging with fruit.

"My brothers," Tylo rolled his eyes. "It's like living in one of those stupid movies where guys do one dumb trick after another, and I've got all the bumps and bruises to prove they're idiots." He rubbed a cut on his forehead. "Got this when Trevor tried to prove a scrap of metal could work as a Frisbee."

"Ouch."

"Tylo!" His mom called, sounding desperate. Who wouldn't, traveling with that crew?

"Gotta go," he shouted, at a run toward his family.

"Later!" I yelled after him.

Just then Mem came back, asking, "Brussels sprouts for lunch?"

I snarled at her. She knew I hated those things, almost as much as I hated spinach, and she cooked that, too.

"All right, how about prunes? They had nice home-dried fruit." Pep shook the bag as we got into the car.

Dried fruit is like dead fruit. It should never be eaten. "Did you at least get some cherries?"

"No cherries, no watermelon."

"No apples, no bananas."

"No fruit a certain girl likes."

"Why not? " I popped up against the back of their seat.

"You can buy any fruit you want, dear." Mem held up her money pouch. "But *you* have to buy it."

Dropping back into my seat, I said, "Never mind." No fruit, and water everywhere I went. The only good thing about this place had to be that kid Tylo and the promise of a nighttime photo expedition. Hey, we might even get a few shots of bats. And Mem hates bats. Maybe I'll leave pictures of them on her pillow one night. Then we'll see how she feels about facing something she fears.

# TREES

Once we carried the groceries inside, I turned to head out for another mountain trek, but Mem said, "Don't you go rock climbing again. I've seen your knees there, lass. Or what's left to the knees in your new jeans. No more climbing alone."

So I had a few scrapes. Big deal.

Like he read my mind, Pep said, "Yesterday it was just a couple of nicks, but today or tomorrow it could be broken bones. You might fall up there and we wouldn't find you till the vultures started circling."

"Ronan!" Mem dropped her shopping bag onto the counter and covered her heart. "How could you say such a thing?"

"Scare tactic, sweet." He kissed her cheek.

"Well, it scared me more than Kyna. So stop it." She gave his arm a twisting pinch.

"Ow." He rubbed the spot. "Right-oh. Vultures aside, you get my meaning, Kyna?"

"Yes." I rolled my eyes. My parents overreacted to everything. I've scraped my knees worse by climbing a tree. If I didn't show up for lunch at exactly noon, Pep would have Search and Rescue out there faster than Mem could say, "What's their number?"

"Why not check out the woods?" Mem suggested as she started to put the food up.

Giving her a hand, Pep said, "Maybe you can ask that boy you met for a good guide about?"

I headed out, saying, "I can find my own way, thank you very much."

"Go, Girl Guide, go," Pep cheered. They called Girl Scouts "Girl Guides" in Ireland. Who knows why? It's not like we go about guiding people through the woods or something. Not that I couldn't do a great job of that myself. I know what side of the tree moss grows on and how to get my bearings from the stars in a clearing.

I know my way around the woods. With nothing but their leaves, I can name over fifty different kinds of trees even this far from home. I had like twenty of them named by the time I reached this mega cool clearing with a "God's hand" stream of light reaching down into it—one of those bright streaks of sunlight shooting down from a cloud that looks like God's just reaching to give old nature a good pat on the ground for looking so gosh darn pretty.

Had me staring at the rocks looking all craggy, the woodland violets just getting ready to bloom, and the wild strawberries shooting out their tiny white blossoms. Add the blackcap bushes along the rim, and that clearing had all the fixings for a good hideaway. I stepped into the sunlight and *shazam*, I realized God just might have been pointing that clearing out to me, because there on the far side stood the biggest spread-your-limbs-wide-best-thing-for-a-tree-fort old oak I had ever seen. Even had a stubby old pine tree too small to grow in that grand oak's shade right up close, so I could use it like a ladder to reach the lowest branch.

A monkey swing here, a good stretching climb there, and *ta-da*, I stood on a branch big enough to hold a house. Standing in that tree, looking over that clearing, I realized that silly old lake could fill up with rain for a year and still not overflow enough to reach me there. I could picture the floorboards under my feet, a rope railing between those two peace sign branches to the northwest, a hammock between the two goalpost branches to the southeast, a nice chair up against the trunk—a sweet little tree-fort-away-from-tree-fort kind of place. Now this was my kind of vacation house.

Then I heard a noise, a *glug, glug, swoop, swoop*. Oh no, not water. Turning around, I realized this fantastic tree had a view. I'd walked myself right up to a low bluff overlooking the lake. Girl Guide, my bum!

I couldn't even steer clear of the one thing I wanted to avoid.

Spinning around to make my escape, I saw that sunlight stretching into the clearing, touching down on those violets, imagined my little hammock swinging in the breeze. Ah, what could that stupid old lake do to me this far up, anyway?

Didn't even give my mind a chance to think about it, just headed back to the house to see what I could scare up to get started on my new fort.

A quick search of the old stone shed turned up a few good boards. Hit up Pep's traveling tool kit for twine. Borrowed rope from the tarp on the woodpile. Then I used an old blanket for the hammock. By lunch, I had the foundation for a pretty good tree fort.

I couldn't talk about anything else over grilled cheese and tomato soup. Mem and Pep nodded and smiled. During a sandwich-dipping break, Pep asked, "And did you ask the tree for permission to go building that fort?"

I remembered Pep standing below the tree in our backyard, praying before he lashed down the first board of the fort he built for me. Just five at the time, I figured trees could be like people. Why not? I had thought the same thing about the tooth fairy and the Easter bunny.

Now, I wondered why Pep still talked about such things. Didn't he know I was too old to believe that stuff? Then again, those stories were the strongest thing I had in common with Mem and Pep. Except for the water steps. And I'd rather forget all about them.

I put my sandwich down, feeling kind of guilty for forgetting our tree spirit tradition. Felt almost like the time I forgot to tell him about career day at school last year. Everybody had a mem or pep come to talk about what they did for a living. And Pep had a pretty good job as a freelance writer for magazines, but I knew he'd come to class with his jolly green Irish accent and his fairy stories and the kids at school would imitate him for weeks, asking me all sorts of questions about Ireland that I couldn't answer.

It happened after my class heard Mem and Pep talking to my teacher about using artificial instead of real trees for the classroom during the Winter Pageant. They are real nature lovers, my parents. They use post-recycling, environmentally friendly, organic products only. And their motto is to never harm nature. So I guess I didn't really forget about career day. I just stalled a little. Like until the event was over.

Pep moped over that one for weeks, looking all sad and misty each time he asked after my day at school. Guess I made him feel bad. And I didn't want to do that again, so I said, "I forgot. Can you come help me do it after lunch?"

He tilted his head like he had to think about it, then sighed and said, "I think I can fit that into my schedule."

I loved how he said *shed-yule* for schedule. Made me think of a shed just for Christmas, chock-full of presents. The kids in my class may make fun of Irish accents, but it's music to my ears.

"Right-oh!" I shouted with the best Irish brogue I could muster. Mem and Pep laughed, then did their deep-in-the-throat American "No way," like a couple of fog horns. I guess Yanks sounded like bull frogs to them.

After lunch, Pep and I trekked back to the tree. Pep leaned back to take in every branch and leaf, then he patted the wrinkled old trunk. "Grandmother of a tree, this one. Probably nearly two hundred years old. Been here since all these trees were but saplings." He waved to the trees around us. "Probably had a clear view of the mountains in her youth."

I could almost see it—that tree just stretching into sapling height, nothing but grass, rocks, violets, and wild strawberries for miles around, all that nature butting up to those craggy old mountains without a road or a human in sight. Would that be the "good old days" to nature? Sometimes I really did wonder if nature thought for itself.

Pep gave me a wink. "I see that you used twine to tie in the boards like I taught you."

"Nails poison trees," I recited, remembering that lecture from when he built my first tree fort. I had learned a thing or two from Pep. And it felt pretty good to be there with him, asking for the tree's permission to build my fort in its branches. The early peoples of the world always respected nature—the Druids of Pep's homeland, the Mohawks of New York, even the Bantus of Africa that we'd studied in school. And since many of their people still believe in the spirits of nature today, why should I find it odd that Pep did? No good reason, I guess.

And as we worked the day away, building and making trips into the woods or to town for this or that to make a nice old fort, I began to think this summer in New York might not be so bad after all.

# TEARS

That night, I slept in my own room, knowing Mem and Pep would go back to the lake after I fell asleep. Couldn't put them this close to water without expecting to see them go for a dip. And if I had my fort, then they should be able to do a bit of swimming.

I tried to sleep with the sound of the waves lapping away down below. Even did it for a little while, thanks to Kippers' purring. Then Mem and Pep showed up in my doorway, whispering with some woman I didn't know. I kept my eyes closed and didn't move so they'd think I was still asleep, but I could hear them as clearly as if they'd whispered in my ear.

"Here she is, Rosien," Mem whispered. Rosien? That's an Irish name.

"She's a real cutie," the woman said, but she didn't sound like she believed it.

Her accent had me itching to jump out of bed. She sounded Irish with her echoing "cue" for cutie. That meant she came from Ireland. Might even have known Mem and Pep in their Irish days. What if she was mates with Mem when they were kids? Wow. Bubble-blowing-wow. Finally, somebody who'd clue me in on their past.

I had to hold my breath to keep from letting them know I was eavesdropping, but I so wanted to ask that lady some questions about Mem. What was she like in school? Did she ever do her math homework (because she never helped me with mine)? What kind of bike did she ride? Who did she play with?

If they didn't leave soon, I'd pop like a balloon. The only reason I didn't bolt out of bed was because I knew Mem and Pep wouldn't let her say a word with them standing there. No, I'd wait until I could talk to her alone, then I'd get the real scoop.

As they closed the door and walked away, I felt all cozy warm with the idea of getting the real story about my parents. No more fairy tales or goofy lines about pictures dropped in ponds. Someone would finally tell me about Mem and Pep before they came to the U.S. Mem claimed I wasn't ready for all that "business," as she called it.

One time she sat me in her lap, pulled her long hair over my shoulders, and let me braid it, saying, "You got a bit of your own childhood to deal with before we muddle it up with ours."

"Huh?"

She kissed my cheek. "That fear of yours, it's like a tidal wave, washing out the rest of the world when it takes you over."

"What's that got to do with you as a kid?"

She put her head next to mine and hummed. "What I'm saying, Kyna, is you have enough to deal with. Your mind's about full up with the worry of it. You get yourself past that fear and the whole world will be yours. Including our lives before you came along and cheered them up."

Another bribe. Take a water step and we'll buy you a zoom lens. Get over your fears and we'll talk about our past. Sounded more like blackmail to me!

What was the big secret anyway?

I'd floated plenty of theories. Like maybe they'd grown up as Travelers, the Irish folks who traveled in caravans and never settled in a home. Nothing wrong with that to me. I'd love to live in an RV and see the world. But a lot of people treated them badly, even accused them of being criminals. That got me to wondering if maybe Mem and Pep might be in the witness protection program for testifying against the Irish Mafia or something. I asked Pep about that last month. That's how he found out I'd been sneaking over to our neighbor Mrs. Pengetti's to watch TV. And I got grounded for a week. Too bad it wasn't for the summer. I could've stayed home.

Mem and Pep only let me watch educational TV, but movies can be educational, too. How else would I know about the witness protection program? They sure never talked about it on any Discovery Channel show I've watched.

No regular TV wasn't the only tough rule Mem and Pep lived by. We couldn't even use shampoo unless it had all natural products inside and said right on the bottle that it wasn't tested on animals. And I'm all for making sure animals don't get hurt, but a girl likes to eat a good Twinkie, drink a tasty soda, and watch a little TV every now and again.

I figured Mem and Pep did plenty of those kinds of things back in their kiddy days. That's why they don't talk about it. They don't want me knowing they actually ate food that could turn into clear liquid if you put it in the microwave. That's right. Twinkies melt down into a sticky clear goo. No real food there. None. Yuck.

I bet that's what Mem and Pep had to hide. A normal childhood.

Pft. Wouldn't fool me for much longer. I'd track that woman down and get her to spill the beans—the jelly beans, the polyester pants, and the bright green apple-smelling, totally artificial shampoo Mem probably went through as a kid. She couldn't hide all that from me for long now that I had her Irish friend to track down and ask.

# SECRETS

I got up the next morning with a mission. I'd hike into Plattsburgh and see what I could find out about this Rosien. With a small town, it's easy to get the inside scoop on folks. They published just about everything in our hometown newspaper. The *Perryville Post* even announced who brought what for church picnics. Plattsburgh wasn't that small, but with a name like Rosien, it'd be pretty easy to track her down with a good word search. Too bad Mem and Pep thought the Internet was a way to catch fish or I wouldn't have to walk all the way to town to find some answers.

Grabbing my camera—a photographer's Swiss Army knife in the "always be prepared" department—I left a note to say I went hiking. Actually, I was hiking. Just not in the mountains as Mem and Pep would suppose. To be honest, I'd prefer a hike in the mountains to trudging into town. I kept to the trees because these days traveling roadside is more dangerous than the chance of running into a bear in the woods.

And even though I'd rather be in my nice, safe downtown park on Clark Street far away from a lake, I had to admit that the ferny undergrowth and sky-scratching pine trees of upstate New York weren't half bad. With it being just light, I even heard an owl hoot—probably headed home for a day's rest. Started thinking a shot of an owl in flight might even top my purple hairstreak shot. What if I got it from above rather than below?

The idea almost had me ready to shimmy up a tree for a test run, but I had a mission. One that proved impossible. At the library, I searched the *Plattsburgh Register* online until my eyes blurred, found a Rose, a Rosie, and two Rose Maries, but no Rosien. Even did a Yahoo search of the phone listings in town. Not a one.

I tried "Ireland," "Irish," and "Immigrant" and all I came up with was a stupid Halloween story about the silkies in the lake. Sure, the article was a joke, something fun for the little kids who still believed in fairies and silkies, but why print that kind of stuff in a paper? Newspapers are supposed to print the facts, not the fairy-tale nonsense Mem and Pep tried to feed me. I needed real answers, like who was this Rosien woman who came to our house the night before?

Not sure what else to do, I asked the librarian if she knew a Rosien.

"Row-sheen, you say. That's pretty," she said. "But no, I don't know anyone by that name."

A lot of help she was. I could've kept trying, but I was a little dizzy from all that searching and a lot hungry, so I headed home, hoping Mem and Pep had a big lunch in the works.

All the way there, I kept wondering, who was this Rosien? Not everyone gets their name in the paper, I guess, but it still seemed odd not to catch even one reference to her. That meant she hadn't been married there or gotten a speeding ticket or been to a town meeting or had a daughter win a ribbon at the Clinton County Fair Mem had told me about. A pretty secretive lady this Rosien. Maybe she talked even less about the past than my mem and pep. She might be a Traveler. They like to stay off the radar. Local folks tend to blame things on strangers they don't understand. And I sure didn't understand why Mem didn't tell me she had a friend living up in Plattsburgh. Maybe that's why Mem and Pep really wanted to vacation there—a chance to see some of the folks from their old home. But how was I ever going to know if I couldn't find Rosien?

Not that I thought it'd do me any good, but I planned to ask Mem and Pep once I got home. When I walked into the kitchen, Mem looked like she'd had a "bout of the misties." That's how she described crying. Like it wasn't nothing more than a bit of weather. But it made me sad just to look at her. Sidetracked all my thoughts of hunting down her Irish friend.

And the view from the kitchen made things worse. The room had more windows than walls and every single one of them looked out at that ripply blue lake. Gave me that tipsy, walking-a-rope-bridge kind of feeling, like the kitchen itself went out over the water. I inched to the wall and started pulling down the shades, so I didn't have to look at it.

Pep sighed, but started pulling shades from the other end of the room so I could join Mem at the table. Afraid my impromptu trip had upset her, I said, "You aren't mad at me for going hiking, are you?"

She touched my hand all kind, then slapped it.

"That's for leaving without asking." She sniffled. "But no, that's not what's given me the misties."

"Just in a family feud," Pep said, pouring Mem a cup of tea.

"Ronan," Mem warned as she dashed some salt into her tea.

Too late, he'd already "spilled the milk" as it were. There was no putting it back in the bottle.

"A feud with who?" I asked, slipping into my chair with thoughts on Rosien. Was she a relative? Even better. She'd know everything about Mem.

Mem and Pep echoed each other, both saying, to my surprise, that Mem had a sister named Rosien.

"You have a sister?" I stood up. "You never told me!" Never told me she had one. Never told me this mystery aunt lived in New York. So that's why we came to Plattsburgh. Maybe they'd had a feud, swore never to speak to each other again, but Mem wanted to patch things up. Maybe she wanted to ask Rosien to be my godmother!

Mem looked as flustered as I felt. She spun her spoon so fast she spilled tea onto the table.

Pep sat down between us, patting both of our hands, "Rosien's a package."

"Package" in Pep language meant you had to take

the good with the bad. A person with kindness in her soul, but darkness in what she did.

What dark thing had she done that had made Mem cry? When she came to see me the night before, she didn't sound so thrilled with me. Was I the reason they didn't get on together? The idea made me feel like I had sand under my skin, all scratchy and wrong. "She doesn't fancy me then?"

Mem looked about ready to cry again, her hand even shook as she sipped her tea. I felt so bad for her, I wanted to cry, too. To get into her arms and hug her.

Pep turned to me and leaned in close. "Rosien's not one to fancy folks. And she got to prattling on about being meant to be a mother to the earth not to children. But not your mem, she's wanted to be a mum from the moment I met her."

"On the rocks of a bay so blue, it made her gray eyes glow." I smiled as I repeated a line from the story Pep always told me of their meeting. Mem even chuckled.

"That's right." He looked over his shoulder at Mem. They smiled at each other.

I got up to go to Mem. Putting my hands on her knees, I said, "But it'd be nice to have your sister around, right?" I'd always dreamed of having my own sister, someone I could hang out with. A person who would understand my fears. Help me when they closed in around me.

Mem nodded. "If she wasn't enough to make me want to stuff her tail end with rocks and see her sink to the bottom."

Pep barked, "Mem."

Just the idea had me shivering. Most people could talk about drowning. Joke about it even. But not me. Just the thought of that choking water made me relive it. The wetness of it filling me, stretching my lungs, drowning out the air, and the black waves churning me around as I sank. Deeper and deeper with the pain of the fight for air crushing me. I backed into the wall as my lungs started going at full shutter speed, leaving me no air to breathe.

Mem scooped me up and ran for the front door. She knew a panic attack when she saw one coming—the kind that seized up my muscles and my mind, leaving me quaking and gasping for breath.

Outside the front door, she pointed up at the bushy pine trees. "Look at those trees. Hear the birdies singing. Think that breeze is blowing those clouds?"

I let the wind blow through my hair, took in the piney fresh air. Pines can't grow in water. I'm on dry land. Staring up into branches in the nice, dry sky. I pulled in a good deep breath and imagined I could fly up into the branches with the birds. No more water. No more churning. No more sinking.

Pep came close, whispering into my hair, "That old lake ain't nothing. Just some of that blue Jell-O you Yanks love so much. Nothing more than jiggly blue Jell-O, so it moves with the wind."

A lake of blue Jell-O. That made me laugh, but I cried too. Cried because Mem had a family. A sister who stayed away because of me. Would they be closer if I wasn't such a mess? Wasn't afraid of silly blue Jell-O water?

If only it were that silly. That stupid. That easy to swallow. Then I could make that fear just disappear down my throat.

I imagined myself drinking that lake down a gulp at a time, but my tummy filled up, my neck tightened, and still it looked as though I hadn't even taken a sip out of the thing. I couldn't even beat that darn water in my mind. How could I ever hope to do it in real life?

If I did, would Mem and Pep stop worrying about me? Would Mem patch things up with her sister Rosien? Could they go back to Ireland and see the rest of their family?

It hurt me in a *fist-around-the-heart* kind of way to

know that taking care of me took so much away from Mem and Pep. I wished I could take my biggest water step ever and just walk right into that stupid lake. But wishes are worth no more than a stone and stones make you sink, so there I stood, holding onto Mem's hand, staring at the trees, and wishing they'd never even heard of Lake Champlain.

# LEAVES

Finding out Rosien was a package who hurt Mem stomped out my ideas of tracking her down. She'd probably only tell me lies anyway.

And with my little freak-out, I just wanted to get away for a bit. Let the cold layer of fear in the pit of my stomach just melt away. Felt like disappearing into the woods to "recharge my batteries," as Pep always says.

And Pep sure loved recharging in the lake. He'd pound away at an article for a couple of hours after breakfast, then come charging out of his new office shouting something in Irish. Mem laughed as he flew past and sped down to the dock. I closed my eyes, so I didn't have to see him jump in, but then I watched real close to see him come back to the surface. Then I could let out the breath I'd been holding inside.

Mem preferred a quiet night swim herself. For breaks from the illustrations she had due come August for some save-the-world magazine, she knit. Kippers loved it. He sat at her feet and played with the yarn. But knitting is not my favorite hobby, really. Meant nice knitted afghans to nestle in by the fire, but it also led to jumpers for Christmas, scarves for birthdays, and more doll blankets than I've got dolls.

"Maybe you could knit Rosien a jumper," I suggested as I left for the woods. Anything so that I wouldn't have to wear another one of those bulky, itchy things to school the first day after Christmas vacation. Last year, Bobby Clarkson said I looked like a mutant snowball.

To get my mind off itchy jumpers and mean kids like Bobby Clarkson, I headed for my tree fort, a great camera roost. I sat up there, belly down on the floor, elbows as a tripod and started taking shots—the sunlight streaming down onto the rocks, the woodpecker drilling for bugs, and the squirrels scrambling about in a nutty little scavenger hunt.

I love how photographs are like windows into a piece of nature. And no matter how the seasons change in the place you captured in that window, you can look inside that picture and see just what you saw when you first snapped the shot. It's like you've stopped time. A bit of magic.

But real magic, not foolish leprechauns and fairies and silkies and all those other made-up things Mem and Pep talked about. Little kid stories I outgrew in kindergarten. Now I made magic of my own with a little glass, a little paper, and a good flash.

Whistling pulled me up short. I wanted to keep my tree fort private. A place just for me. The song being whistled didn't have the hop and the jump of one of Pep's tunes, and Mem's not one for woods—too many snakes and bats about for her. What if it was one of Tylo's rowdy brothers? They'd probably try to claim my fort. I had a serious need for some acorns myself, something I could pitch fast and hard to keep them away.

Then I caught sight of the whistler through the trees. From the clam-combed hair, I realized it was Tylo. Eh, he could see my fort. Just as long as he didn't tell his brothers about it. But to play it safe, I got down and headed out to the clearing to meet up with him.

"Hi there," I said as he came closer.

"Hello." He dragged his feet, a canvas bag snagging along behind him.

"What's wrong?"

"My brother Trevor caught me stuffing my green beans in my pocket. Now I have to help him collect leaves for his science project. He has to get a gazillion of them before he goes back to school. Scratch that. I have to find them all. He'll be at the beach all day."

Sibling blackmail. Now there's one thing I'd never miss about not having a brother—

That lie hit me like a bolt of lightning charging right down into my feet. I'd had a brother. An older brother who would've caught me planting my brussels sprouts in the fern by the back door.

To let my brother Kenny know I would've done his science projects, carried his books, and even cleaned his nuclear disaster of a room—if it meant I could have him back—I decided to give Tylo a hand. After all, I knew my leaves.

Pulling off a pine needle, I said, "Here's a white pine to start things off."

"Cool." He rushed forward to grab the needles, popped them in a book in his bag, then rushed for a struggling maple. "Thanks for your help."

Felt good to help him, a faint hint of the kind of things I could've done with my own brother. And Tylo turned out to be a cool kid. Even if he did have a fairy tale obsession with threes. He fancied himself a spelunker and promised to take me to see his favorite caves—all three of them. He had a comic book collection big enough to fill three bookcases. He even had three brothers and three loose teeth (thanks to his youngest brother, Ben, who tripped him into a rock).

"It's okay, they're all baby teeth." He pushed them with his tongue. "Do you think I could get enough from the tooth fairy to buy that special night film you were talking about?"

"You mean your mom and dad? The tooth fairy isn't real."

I knew the score on fairies. All the fairy stories of my childhood had sent me in search of those little critters. I'd found a book about them at school. Told me everything from the myths about the hill-living baby-stealers to those famous doctored-up photographs that had people in England believing those little woodland pixie types might actually be real. Yeah, right. About as real as Gaylen Parker's sunset. Not only did that book show me how people could fix photographs, but it also taught me that all those magical, fantastic stories Mem and Pep had told me didn't have a word of truth in them.

Reading that book made me feel like I'd been

living inside a beach ball and someone sucked all the air out and left me with just a shrunk-up blob of plastic. All the possibilities of fairies and pixies and pookas just shriveled right up. That's why I preferred real, honest, taken-from-life pictures that showed what a person can see, hear, and touch. They captured the real world.

And that's what I wanted from Mem and Pep—the real truth about their childhood. But instead I get to learn the ins and outs of fairyland. They can keep it.

But Tylo seemed like the type of kid who'd still clap for Tinkerbell to say he believed in fairies. He stopped and squinted at me. "Does that mean you don't believe in any imaginary things?"

I walked past him. "Why would I, if they're imaginary?" That'd be like waiting up to catch Santa eating the cookies you've left when you could be eating those cookies yourself.

"What's just make-believe to some people is real to others, like those people who can see ghosts."

"Mediums?" I laughed. "They're just pretending."

"People aren't always pretending when they see imaginary things."

I kept walking, searching for a birch tree, so it took me a minute to notice that he hadn't followed me. I turned to see him standing there with the bag on his shoes, his head down, his shoulders all droopy like he'd just found out Santa Claus was a hoax.

Sad feelings are like a shrinking potion. When someone I like, even a new friend like Tylo, feels bad, it shrinks me up inside.

"Okay." I shrugged. I didn't really believe him, but I had to say something to cheer him up. I thought about the article I'd seen on silkies in the town paper and I blurted out, "My parents say there are silkies in this lake."

You'd think I'd lit a rocket in his shoes the way he came rushing forward all shouts and laughter. "They do? That's what I think, too! Lots of people around here joke about them. But I saw one three nights ago. Tried to take its picture, but the picture didn't turn out. If you used your camera and that film you're talking about, we could get one on film!"

His words blew up a balloon of laughter in my mouth, but I couldn't let it out. He'd know I thought he was a goofus.

Silkies? Even my leprechaun-loving parents didn't really think they lived in that lake. Those were just wacky stories people tell. Tylo probably just saw fish jumping in the water, not a ship-guiding seal. I coughed to let my laughter out, then said, "If you want that film, you'd better talk to your brother."

"Why?"

"Three teeth won't get you enough money to buy it."

His eyes got so big his head kind of flopped back like they made it too heavy. He thought I was serious. A total goofus.

But I liked goofuses. How else would I put up with Pep? Giving Tylo a shove, I said, "Just kidding," then headed on to find more leaves.

"Well, I've got to get that picture." He shook his head. "My brothers just won't shut up about me seeing a silkie. They keep calling me 'Gully.'" He turned to me. "That's for 'gullible,' as in a kid so dumb he'd believe the moon is made of cheese."

He kicked a tree. "I don't think that." Picking at the bark, he said, "I saw that silkie, Kyna. I really did."

His sadness seeped inside me and felt familiar. The kids at school made me feel that way all the time. What with my aversion to anything watery and a bobbing-for-apples mishap that I'm too ashamed to even think about, I knew the soul-squashing feeling of having kids tease you. I had to help Tylo prove to his brothers that he had seen something in that lake.

Maybe not a silkie, but something. So I said, "I could take the picture if we get the film."

"Maybe I could sell a comic book. I have a few double copies I could part with. Do you like Spiderman?"

He followed me into the woods and we made plans to buy the film and take pictures of silkies or flopping fish or whatever showed up.

# TEA

I came home to find my Aunt Rosien sitting at our kitchen table, petting Kippers and sipping tea. "Afternoon to ya." She held her cup up to me, her hair as red and curly as Mem's was gray and straight. Didn't look like Mem's sister to me.

"Afternoon." I stood by the door, waiting to see what she'd do.

"Your pep's on the horn with his editor and Itha's getting all that paint off her hands. Stuff's toxic, you know. Kills the fish when they dump the cans in the water. Hate the stuff, myself."

"Mem wouldn't dump it in the water." Mem mixed her own paints to use as many natural things as she could.

"Right." She sighed. Great, I'd annoyed her already. I figured I'd be better off leaving her alone, so I turned to go.

"What you got there?" She pointed at my hand.

I twirled the leaf I held. "Just something I picked with a friend."

"If you were a fish, how'd you feel if I pulled off a scale?"

"What?"

"Same thing as taking a leaf, you know? It's a living thing, that tree. You couldn't wait until the leaf fell?"

Pep's comment about Aunt Rosien being an Earth Mother popped into my head. And she was really protective of her "child," all right. I thought Mem and Pep were nature nuts. If so, then Aunt Rosien had to be a nature freak. I'd heard of people getting mad when you nailed a sign to a tree. And I do, too. Nails poison trees when they rust, but a leaf? Every tree has thousands. Like they'd miss one. But I bet a fish has that many scales, too. Would it hurt when you took one off? Like having your hair pulled out? I shuddered to think about it.

"What are you telling her?" Mem asked as she came in just in time to see me shudder. She rubbed my back.

"Fish are dying from paint cans thrown in the water

and trees don't appreciate it when you pluck off their leaves." Rosien took a sip. An honest one, that aunt of mine. Maybe she would tell me true stories about Mem.

"Lovely. Nice to meet you too, Auntie." Mem went to the stove for a cup of her own. "Don't mind her, Kyna. She'd tell the sun it shined too hot on turtles. Gave them tough skin."

They both laughed. Rosien nodded. "Aye, I did say that when I was a girl."

Seeing her laugh made me imagine she'd opened a small door. I might be able to sneak through if I was careful. Maybe even learn what kind of things Mem said when she was little.

Sitting down, I prepared for a trade—a story for a story. I'd tell her about me, then maybe she'd tell me about Mem. "When we lived in an apartment, the landlord knocked a bird nest out of the air conditioner unit by our balcony. So Pep and I made a tree out of a coat rack and fabric-covered coat hangers for leaves and left all of the fixings for a new nest."

Rosien leaned over the table to have a close listen in. "Did it work?"

"Yep, four babies." I held up my fingers. "One of them had three brown spots on its head when it flew away. We had a pep bird with three spots on its head the very next year." Those little birdie families made it easier to wait to move back into my grandma's house. After the sea took my family, I had to live in a foster home for the six months it took Mem and Pep to get licensed as foster parents. Then came the long, drawn-out wait for the adoption to become final. With no will, it took nearly two years for the courts to decide Gram's little house could belong to Mem and Pep until I was old enough to claim it. After all, no one else could. Gram's only brother died in the Vietnam War, and she didn't have any other children besides my dad. And Mom was an orphan like me. At least I had Mem and Pep, and now an aunt. Even one as grouchy as Aunt Rosien was a good thing.

"Glory to the stars," Aunt Rosien smiled and patted her knee. "Now that's a fine story." She looked at Mem who came to the table with her tea.

"And it's true," Mem said, smiling.

"Even better."

I smiled to see that Aunt Rosien salted her tea like Mem and Pep did.

Stirring a little sugar into my cup, I asked, "So, did Mem rescue any animals?"

Rosien's face stretched into a smile of surprise. "Now how'd you know she did that?"

An animal shows up in our yard and Mem finds it

a home whether it has wings, fur, or scales. She even found a home for a blind, albino squirrel. With a record like that, she would've had to start young.

Mem blew on her tea, saying, "She doesn't need to hear any of that."

"Oh?" Rosien asked, then nudged me saying, "Your mem would've started her own zoo for all the critters she dragged in—otters, seagulls, even brought home a three-legged turtle."

I laughed, imagining Mem, all pigtails and pretty dresses, dragging home one animal after another. Leave it to Mem to be bringing home sea critters. I bet she combed every beach, the way she loved the water.

"Aye, our Mem thought Itha wanted a wee baby to care for, so she had our brother, Shannon."

"A boy named Shannon?" I had an uncle?

"Wasn't no name for a girl till you Yanks started messing with it."

Felt like I should apologize, but I said, "Where's Shannon now?"

"Ireland," Mem jumped in, all smiles. "Lad's studying to be an oceanographer."

"Cool . . ." Wow an uncle too? Man, I might even have a couple cousins, but they probably love the water like the rest of the clan.

Rosien grumbled into her tea, but Mem quickly said, "And what I'd like Rosien to tell us is how she made that jumper she's wearing." Mem gave it a tug. A mossy green, it hung low at the cuffs and had a loose weave that made it "drape," as Mem called it. What I'd like to know is why anyone would want a jumper that looked like drapes? It's not like you'd hang it in a window, right?

Besides, I wanted to know more about Mem's family, not how to knit. But Mem brought out the yarn and the two of them set to clicking their needles and chattering in Irish, laughing and teasing until I felt about as useful as a toe next to a thumb. Right about then, I decided it would be good to try my hand at mapping a few of the trails through the woods around the house. If I did a good enough job, made my own signs to mark the trails, maybe even cleared a trail or two of my own, I might just be able to finish that Get With the Land project after all.

But I didn't get much further than a few squiggly lines, because I kept thinking about little girl Mem traipsing home with her wee found pets. Why couldn't she share her true stories with me? Just 'cause it's true doesn't mean a real story could hurt me. Could it?

# HAIR

When I came back that evening and saw the two of them still sitting at the table, I figured Mem and her sister had worked out a little truce over their knitting. But their battle resumed when Aunt Rosien left. They'd been talking about recipes when they walked out of the kitchen. Then I heard Aunt Rosien say, "Well, you know, Itha, it's a duty, not a vacation attraction. You can't just come up here to enjoy yourself for a while, then leave."

"I'm well aware of my duties, Rosien."

I tried to keep cleaning up the kitchen, but the anger in Mem's voice froze me still. Besides, Mem spoke true. A Sierra Club president back home, she planted trees every month instead of once a year, and there's no one who lived farther from the ocean who did more to preserve it. She even took trips to Washington to lobby the government guys to save the critters of the deep. Mem did a lot for the earth, but Rosien didn't seem convinced.

"Really now, is that why you're up here lounging about in this house while I'm down doing my duty?"

What kind of duty? Did they have some endangered species in the lake I didn't know about? A sand turtle with nowhere to lay eggs or a type of fish dying of paint poisoning?

Mem turned and headed back up the steps, saying, "I have a job of my own to do. And there's more than one kind of duty, sister. More than one."

She came into the kitchen with her head hanging low, so I made a big show of clanking the tea pot as I washed it so she'd think I'd made too much noise to hear them fight. Knowing the duty she'd just referred to included me, I realized I took her away from whatever cause Rosien wanted her to fight for.

Mem came to join me. We finished the dishes in silence, then she pulled her downy hair out of the bun on top of her head, saying, "I think this old mane could use a bit of brushing. What do you say?"

I'd say I loved to brush Mem's hair. She had the only true gray hair I'd ever seen on a person's head. Not white gray like that of a grandma, but the rich gray of a black-footed mare. Down to the backs of her knees, Mem had hair long enough to hide me when she brushed it forward and let me sit on her lap.

We'd spooked Pep that way many a time. Mem would hide me away, then keep combing. Pep would come into the room for a good night's rest. I'd pop out, shouting, "Wooo!"

One time, I scared him as he walked in to watch a movie and it rained popcorn. "Aye, you little banshee. I'll have that howl of yours." He chased me around the bed three times before he caught me and tickled me until I nearly wet the bed.

And you could say I had memories in that hair of Mem's—all the times I sat on the high bed behind her vanity bench to brush it. We'd talk and laugh until my arm got tired, then she'd pull the hair over her shoulder and finish the job while I played with her hair combs or made chains of her bobby pins.

But that night, it flowed like cement over her shoulders, keeping a wall between us. She sighed, but said nothing as I started to brush. Tall enough now, I stood behind her and brushed out the long strands.

Kippers snuck down below to play with the tips.

Mem kept silent, so I grabbed a chunk of her hair and pretended to rat it out a little. "What a beautiful tail. Our little gray mare is bound to win the show." Usually that gave her a laugh, but this time she barely hummed.

I didn't feel much happier. Sad because Aunt Rosien made Mem sad, but also guilty for listening in on what they said. And a little angry, too. Why did Mem have to hide her childhood from me when we could've shared stories like the one Rosien had told me over tea?

"Mem," I started.

"Aye?" Mem sounded distant, even drifty.

"What's wrong with telling me about those critters you rescued?"

Mem looked at me in the mirror, her eyes all flash and wonder. "And just where do you think I rescued them? That otter with a crushed foot and the eel with the fish hook in its eye?"

I blinked, my own eye stinging. In a flash, I could see Mem, her skirts tied in knots over her knees, wading into the water to help an otter trapped in the rocks, the poor thing letting out high-pitched squeals, splashing in the water to get free. Felt the water splatter me. Wiped the idea of it off me in a hurry.

Mem turned to take my hands and steady them. "Most days, you couldn't catch me out of the water, Kyna. My childhood's filled with water. You want to hear stories about water?"

I pulled away, shaking my head.

She brought me back into a silky hair hug. "That's what I thought."

What an idiot. All this time, I thought Mem and Pep had been keeping secrets, but as always, they only wanted to protect me. To save me from my own stupid fears. Why did I still have to be so afraid of water? Why couldn't I just dissolve it down to nothing and live like everybody else? Mem could tell me all about her life on the Irish coast. We could swim together. Laugh as we splashed in the water.

Just thinking about it brought a burst of memory laughter into my head. *I could feel the sun on my face, see beads of water flying in the air, hear a child laughing. Was it me? Did I see a beach and a woman half-turned, splashing in a bright white suit with berry red dots?*

Who was that lady? It couldn't have been Mem, she didn't own a berry dot suit. I hadn't gone near water since, since . . . when I thought of that awful day on the boat, I realized just who it could be. Mom. I'd remembered my mom. Just a smiling woman in a picture to me on most days. I closed my eyes to hold onto the feeling of her. Then I remembered the photograph of my mom and me sitting on a dock, me in a frilly pink suit and purple floaters on my arms, her in a sail white suit with little red dots.

Mem tapped my nose. "A memory got you?"

I smiled, feeling the warmth of it just flowing through me like hot milk on a cold night. "Yeah."

"Well, there's proof water can be a good thing. In my childhood and yours." She gave me a squeeze.

Maybe so. But my memories of life with my first family are just flashes, broken pieces of sound and half pictures. I didn't have any real good memories of water. Just that one awful memory. I had to hold my breath to keep it away.

Mem tapped me with the brush. "No falling down on the job there, lass. Get to brushing. This hair won't let go of its tangles without a fight."

"Yes, ma'am." I saluted, knowing Mem tried to distract me. And I needed it or I'd sink back into the dark memory of a watery world with no air.

So I set to brushing and forcing myself to think of other things. But my mind had fallen into a bit of a rut. I went from one bad memory to another, recalling Aunt Rosien storming off down the steps leading to the lake.

Had my mind spinning with the worry of why she might be mad at Mem.

"Why was Aunt Rosien so mad when she left?"

Mem closed her eyes and relaxed her shoulders—a sign she meant to keep Rosien's anger from settling inside her. "Sometimes sisters see things a bit different. Rosien sees her duty to the lake."

So it was something to do with saving the lake or the critters that lived there. "She's a conservationist?"

Mem laughed. "I'd say she is. I do my bit when I can, but I see my greatest duty as being a mother to you."

Why did keeping the lake clean and safe have to be so important that a person couldn't have a family, too? Maybe Rosien just took it all a little too seriously. And that's what made her a "package." After all, she was a lady who thought it was wrong to pick leaves. But it still didn't feel right, so I asked, "Aunt Rosien thinks you should be saving the lake instead of raising me?"

Mem pulled me into her lap to give me a neck nuzzle, which made me laugh. "Well bosch on her if she can't see all I've gained in raising you, my sweet."

"Like what?" I asked, seeing us in the mirror. Mem's hair flowed over the both of us like strands of kelp, her eyes shone so dark and round, mine all blue and spinky.

"Like a darn good hair brusher for one thing." She rubbed my head with the brush.

I laughed. "No, really."

Squeezing me, she said, "Selfish as I am, it's the growing that means the most to me, really."

"That I get taller?" I teased.

She spun me over in her lap to tickle me. "That you get stronger and smarter and prettier every day!" I squirmed and laughed and she gave me nose kisses until I believed every word and went to bed happy.

# WAVES

When the snap of the screen door woke me up, I figured Mem and Pep were headed for their nightly swim. Walking toward the front of the house, I could hear their laughter as they ran down the steps that lead to the shore. Made me think of their first night swim together in that cove near Dublin. Seemed so unfair that they loved something I feared so much. That made their nightly swim as private and unreachable as the memory I could never share. I stood in an empty house afraid to go near the water, knowing Mem and Pep laughed and splashed and jumped from the rocks like a couple of first graders.

Loneliness opened up inside me like a yawn. If I ever hoped to swallow that terrible feeling, I had to force myself to go near the water. Get inside it even.

Doing nothing meant standing alone in an empty house. Avoiding other kids who might ask me to swim. Never going to birthday parties during pool season. Turning into a loony if someone even mentioned something that might make me think of going under water. Like the Halloween party last year.

Bobby Clarkson came up with the stupid idea of bobbing for apples. He kept saying, "See it's easy. Look." He plunged his head in. My lungs shrank up and my muscles went as hard as one of those apples as I closed my eyes and prayed he'd come up. He threw his head back, flinging water everywhere. It splashed me and felt like hot sparks against my skin. I brushed it off and screamed as I ran for the door.

Then came the waves of laughter, all the kids in my class shouting and taunting, "Kyna's afraid of water! Water baby!"

I ran straight down the hall and right out the front door. I didn't even stop to catch my breath until I'd run the six blocks home. And as soon as the ache in my lungs stopped, I charged up to the top floor of our house and hid under my own bed. So much for fourth grade. I never wanted to go back.

Mem and Pep went to the school and talked to Mrs. Morton, who had the brilliant idea of telling my whole class how my family died. Every kid wrote me a letter to apologize. In the lunch line, Bobby Clarkson gave me his P.S. saying, "Too bad your parents are dead," like it was nothing worse than losing a library book. I hate that kid.

And I hate always having to be scared. Afraid of a flushing toilet. Or a bubbling fountain in a park. Or of going with my own family to a stupid farmers' market just because it's cozied up to a stupid lake. The more I thought about it, the madder I got. Mad enough to pound rocks into dust.

Water wouldn't chase me out of my own life anymore. I'd chase it. Push it back. Watch it dry up in the sun. Yeah, I'd face that stupid lake.

Stepping outside, I stood on the porch, Kippers winding his way between my legs. Felt the moistness of the night air on the wood of the railing. Didn't let it bother me, just walked down to the wispy grass.

Standing there, I listened to the water. Heard Mem whisper in my ear, "Just think of it as a nice, smooth swing rocking in the wind—*up, then back, up, then back.* Nothing to fear. You always know it's coming."

*Up, then back, up, then back.* I imagined myself on our patio swing back home, Mem beside me, her arm over my shoulder, keeping me safe.

Inching my way to the top of the first step, I wished the railing came into our yard. I grabbed the rail as I eased my foot onto the next step. Then a wild wave froze me halfway between steps as it crashed into the rocks below. I imagined Mem saying, "Just the swing getting a little riled." But I hated the lurching twist of a swing pushed too hard.

Taking a deep breath, I reminded myself that the water couldn't reach me that high up on the shore. Put both feet firm on the ground. I closed my eyes and stood there without prickling up. My skin felt calm. My muscles felt loose. I could even breathe like normal. Felt a hint of good seeping into me.

Then the air changed a little, got a bit thicker, even wetter. A bit spooked, I opened my eyes to see Mem and Pep standing on the steps below me, staring. Their eyes looked gray and glassy in the moonlight.

"Kyna?" Mem asked as if to say, "Where are you headed?"

"I, I . . ." I couldn't tell them about my little private water war. Giving away the secret would mean they'd force me to keep my word. They'd never let me back out. Pointing to a tree, I said, "I just wanted to know if you'd buy me some night film. I'm going to take a picture of an owl in flight."

"Are you, now?" Pep asked, looking like he only half-believed me.

It would make a pretty good picture, but film had nothing to do with why they'd found me there.

As they walked toward me, ignoring just where they'd found me, they stood on either side of me, so we could all go into the house together. Mem said, "Sounds like a plan to me. Maybe you could capture a shot of one of those great horned owls. I love them."

"Have wingspans the length of a kayak, they do." Pep said, heading to the stove.

"Can eat a skunk, those owlies can," Mem said.

"Must give them powerfully bad breath," Pep added.

We laughed, then shared a cup of cocoa before bed, dropping a marshmallow down for Kippers to bat about. I could tell by the way they brushed my hand, looked at me over their steamy cups, and tucked me into bed for a little too long that Mem and Pep knew just what a big water step I'd taken that night. Their pride made me feel hot cocoa warm all over. I fell asleep believing I might even be able to take the next step.

# WOODS

My owl story had all the fixings. It gave me a need for night film. A good goal for my county fair picture. And a reason to be out at night with Tylo, who wanted that picture to shut his brothers up. Of course, Mem and Pep insisted on meeting him before they let us trolly off into the woods.

Tylo stood by the kitchen table, decked out like he'd just stepped out of a tomb-raiding video game—all shoulder-strap pouches, binoculars, and adventuring garb from his brown hat to his hiking boots.

Pep squinted at him. "You look pretty well outfitted."

Tylo tugged on his straps. "Yep."

"Got drinking water, have you?"

"Yep," Tylo tapped on his canteen.

"Torch?"

"In the woods?" Tylo asked, shocked.

Smirking, I told Tylo, "He means a flashlight."

"Oh," Tylo nodded. "Yep." He turned it on and off, nearly blinding Pep.

With a leer, Pep teased, "Glow in the dark compass?"

Tylo patted his chest pocket. "Yep."

Mem and I laughed to see Pep stifle a look of surprise.

"And what do you do if you get lost?"

"Scream until someone comes and finds us?"

Pep curled his nose in disgust. "No."

Tylo laughed and gave Pep a shove. "I know." He held up a walkie-talkie. "It's got a ten-mile radius. Five in the woods. Beeps when it's out of range, so when I hear it beep, I turn around."

Pep nodded, impressed. "And your mem has the other one?"

"Mem?"

"Mom," I told him.

"Yep." Tylo nodded, looking a little confused. He didn't expect that meeting my parents would require a translator.

Once Tylo had written down his number so they

could reach Tylo's mom if they needed to, Pep finally agreed that Tylo was ready for the woods and let us go.

I grabbed Tylo by the shoulder and pushed him toward the door. "Let's head out. I want to catch an owl while it's still hunting. I don't want to see it actually catch anything."

"Owls?" he asked as I pushed him onto the porch.

Luckily, Mem and Pep were shouting, "Happy hunting!" too loud to hear him.

Heading off the deck, I told him, "Owls are my cover story, so don't blow it."

"I thought your parents knew about the silkies?"

"They do." Drat, I'd trapped myself. If I told Tylo why I needed a reason to be on the steps the night before, then he'd find out I'm afraid of water. And there'd go another friendship. But wait, I had a way out. "You didn't want them to come with us, did you?"

"Nooo." Tylo shook his head as he headed for the steps to the beach.

He raced down them like they were nothing more than the stairs that got him from his bedroom to his breakfast.

Seeing him get closer to the water, I froze up. "Hey, Tylo."

He stopped.

"Owls don't go down there." Okay, so *I* couldn't go down there, but the owl excuse had worked so far.

"Right." Tylo spun around and ran back up.

Felt lighter to have him up at the top with me. We headed into the woods.

As I followed him through the trees, I struggled to find a way to keep us away from the water, but close enough to photograph his jumping fish-silkies. The need to keep the camera dry would keep me out of the water, but not off the beach.

Beaches freaked me out. Not only did they border the water, but the suck-in-your-feet sand pulled you down if you stood in one place too long. Tylo had complained about all the rocks on the beach, but rocky beach or not it was still too close to the water. I could feel the moisture in the air like liquid mold on my skin and smell the rotting weeds. Yuck!

But wait. Smell—yeah, that was it. "Hey, Tylo."

"Yeah?"

"I hear silkies can smell as well as they can see."

Tylo kept walking, but he shouted over his shoulder, "They can see underwater, even in the dark."

"Well, did you know they can smell you from a hundred yards away?"

"Oh, man!" He said it with a heavy bummer accent.

"And my mom made me wear this stinky bug spray."

If we could get up high enough, I'd be fine. Heights didn't scare me, just water. And if we could watch from above, I could convince myself the black water was nothing more than wheat moving in the night wind. High. That's it. My tree fort would be perfect!

Tylo stared at his bangs, trying to think.

"I've got some place." I grabbed him and started to drag him to the clearing. We made it there before I got my first bug bite. Now, that's what I call trailblazing.

The moon lit up the clearing all glittery blue. Made the climb up easy.

Tylo asked, "You build this?"

"Me and Pep." Felt good to say that.

"Cool. But how can we see a silkie from here?"

I pulled his binoculars up to his eyes then pointed through the branches.

"Mega-cool," he said, leaning out.

I held my breath, then snuck a peek. In the dark, even with the full moon, the sway and swash of water just looked like wind wooshing wheat around if I squinted my eyes just right. Crouching down on the floor Pep and I had lashed down, I could hear the waves below, but I just gave the swing in my head a push and kept calm—*up, then back, up, then back*—no problem.

Lying down, Tylo brought out his goodies— brownies and bug juice (aka Kool-Aid). We were set for a night of silkie spotting.

But all we saw poking up out of the water were rocks, rocks, and more rocks.

"Did you know that silkies can come ashore and take their pelts off like a robe?" Tylo asked, smooshing brownie bits to his teeth.

Know it? I'd heard the story so many times I repeated the second half without even thinking. "And if someone finds their pelt where they've hidden it on the beach, the silkies are doomed to walk on dry land as a human for the rest of their lives."

"Yeah," Tylo frowned as he licked his teeth. "I guess they die of sadness."

Or they would if they existed. But luckily, Tylo never got a chance to test my belief in silkies, because the bushes to the south of the beach started to shimmy.

"Look," Tylo whispered in my ear. "It might be a silkie trying to return to the water."

Jumping fish didn't start in the bushes, so I asked, "You saw them come out of the bushes?"

"No," he pointed toward the water. "I saw them jump off those rocks."

*More like over them*, I thought, looking at the boulder peninsula he pointed to.

"Here they come." He nudged me as the bushes rustled again.

Out of the bushes waddled two raccoons, a mama and a papa followed by babies make five. A little food-washing lesson, I bet.

"Wow," I put on my amazed voice and started taking pictures. "The rare ring-tailed silkies. Who would believe it?"

"Shut up!" He gave me a shove. He was a shovey kind of kid. Must be from having so many brothers.

The raccoon family washed their meal, then moved on. We switched back to our thrilling rock watch until Tylo started to do the potty squirm. I had to go, too, but I wasn't going to squirm around like a snake with its tail caught in a trap.

"Be right back," Tylo scurried down to the ground. It's pretty convenient to have ready-made bathrooms behind every tree. But I'm not a big fan of leaf toilet paper. That'd really make Aunt Rosien mad.

Tylo came back up, then started dumping canteen water on each hand.

I held my breath, watching the water gush over his hand, hearing the lake lapping at the shore down below. I started sinking below sea level in my mind's eye. If I didn't get a handle on it, I'd pull a freak-out and Tylo would never want to see me again. Oh come on, Kyna, it's just water. A little wash up, as Pep would say.

But I'd already backed up and Tylo had started staring at me, so I had to talk fast. "I've seen enough rocks. Let's go home."

Startled, Tylo dropped his hands, saying, "Now? Can't we stay a little longer? They came last night. Why couldn't you have come last night?"

"We had to go to Albany for the night film," I told him, breaking the last brownie in half to share it with him.

"Well, maybe they'll be back tomorrow." He looked so sad, I almost gave him my half, too. "Will you come back tomorrow? I can bring more brownies."

"Sure, I'll bring some Irish biscuits."

"Biscuits?" He frowned.

"They're cookies, silly."

"Oh." He stuffed his half into his cheek, then said, "Okay."

We headed back through the woods. We said our good-byes at the edge of my yard, then headed for home. Seeing him disappear into the trees made me a little nervous. "Hey, Tylo!"

"Yeah?" He called back, but I couldn't see him.

"How about you give me your walkie-talkie and then call me when you get home?"

Tylo came back. "You know, my dad used to say that worrying is in a woman's genes." He laughed. "I used to think he meant jeans with a 'j.' So when my mom wore jeans, I asked her to show me her worries. She gave me lint. I put it in a box in the stand by my bed. I thought it'd make her worry less. But she still worried a lot. Then my brother told me about genes with a 'g,' so now I know what Dad meant." He handed me the walkie-talkie. "Here you go, Worry Genes." He laughed and walked back into the woods.

"Good night, Lint Boy," I called after him.

"Yadda, yadda."

"Be quiet or I'll track you down and steal all of your leaves."

He stopped. "Just try getting past my brother."

"I'll send a fairy after him. She'll cart him off to a fairy hill and you'll never see him again."

There was a pause, then Tylo's voice came back, "Sounds good to me!"

I laughed. "Good night, Tylo."

"Good night."

Heading back to my room, I realized Tylo had

been right, I was a Worry Genes. I worried that Tylo would get lost and he didn't have the walkie-talkie to call for help. Worried that he'd fall into a hole in the dark and be trapped there all night. Petting Kippers to keep calm, I still couldn't stop spinning scary maybes until the staticky pop of the walkie-talkie made me jump out of my deck chair.

"Back safe, Worry Genes."

"Good night, Lint Boy."

"Good night."

# WORRY

Sitting on the deck in the dark, I started thinking about the lint Tylo collected from his mom. He did it so she'd worry less. That's *breakfast-in-bed* nice. Not me. I made my mem worry more with all of my fears and freak-outs.

I could take another water step to change that. Face that water down. And wash her worries away.

With Rosien giving her grief, Mem deserved a little worry lift. So I forced myself to do more than walk down those steps onto that beach. This time I'd go into the water. Walk straight into my fear.

Keeping my eyes on the trees, I marched right for the steps to the beach. One step. Two step. Three. Then

I heard a noise, an echo-off-the-water bark. Like a dog on a dock. Stopped me cold. Did I really hear that?

Splash! Something hit the water. Did somebody pitch balls off their dock for a dog at night? Was that what Tylo had seen the night before?

Mystery solved. And if I got a picture of the dog, Tylo could prove he'd seen something in the water after all. And a strange something at that. Not too many dogs went diving after dark.

I had to test this theory.

My little quest pulled me like an anchor to the rock line of the beach. Scanning the water, I searched for the dog that made the sound. But I saw nothing. No dog. Not even a ripple in the water.

But Mem and Pep had to have gone swimming. They always did. Why couldn't I see them? Why couldn't I hear them? Seeing only the inky black water filled me with a slimy sense of dread. I tried to wash it down with a hope to myself that they must've come ashore. I scanned the beach, the rocks in the water, even the dock floating way out. No Mem. No Pep. Where could they be?

# ROCKS

"Mem! Pep!" I jumped onto a big rock to get a better view. Nothing. "Mem! Pep!" I jumped to the next rock, screaming for them. Running, I leapt from rock to rock, calling out. Did they go back up? No, they would've passed me on the stairs. Did they go farther down the beach to swim somewhere new?

No one swam like Mem and Pep. No way could they've drowned.

But my birth father sailed Tierra del Fuego and he drowned.

"Mem! Pep!" I screamed so hard my voice cracked and all I could do was whelp out a croak. Fear tumbled like rocks through my chest. Oh God, please keep them safe. Mem called him the Good Giver because he gave everything life. Now I prayed he'd give them back to me.

But what if he didn't?

I felt the panic coming on like a tidal wave. It'd wash me clean out of the here and now.

What good would I be to Mem and Pep then?

*Hold it back, Kyna. Keep your wits.*

To calm down, I started to repeat all of the first aid I could remember from the lessons I took while other kids learned to swim. *To give CPR, check for response, give rescue breaths, and pump.* As I looked up I found myself on the other end of our beach. Still no sign of them.

Seeing a neighbor's steps, I ran for them. I had to call for help.

"Kyna!" Mem shouted from behind me.

Spinning, I saw her waving from the rocky point to the south. "Here, sweet. We're here!" Pep crawled up behind her. Was he pulling on his trunks?

Embarrassed, I faced the shore and covered my face. My fear crashed into a wave of anger before falling into a sea of embarrassment. My parents had gone skinny dipping. I could've melted. I ran for our own steps and didn't stop until I got to my room.

My nerves kept me pacing, flipping my emotions back and forth—one second scared enough to cry, the next so embarrassed I could've hidden under my bed for a week. My parents had been swimming in the lake without any clothes on. Teenagers did that. Not parents!

"Kyna!" Pep shouted, charging into the house.

I couldn't talk to him. Or even look at him. I thought he might be drowning or lost or whatever! And he was . . . oh, I didn't even want to think about it.

I heard him pound up the steps. He threw open the door like the house had caught fire and he had to get me out.

Even in his trunks, I kept thinking about what he'd been wearing a little bit ago. Or not wearing. Facing the wall, I said, "Did you have to?"

Mem rushed into the room, panting.

"Have to . . . ?" Pep asked, confused.

"What? What'd she say?" Mem wanted to know.

I stared at my feet. "Skinny dipping? Did you have to? What if Tylo's mom saw you?" They did live south of us. And I bet his mom stayed up until he got home. If she'd seen them, she'd never let Tylo come over to my house again.

Silence. Then Mem and Pep started to laugh.

"This isn't funny!" I spun to face them, ready to knock their heads together.

Mem stared to speak, but only sputtered.

Pep swallowed to catch his breath, then said, "Kyna, no one can see us. We swam too far out. No yard lights. No boats. Just us."

"And our birthday suits." Mem posed like she showed off a new outfit.

"What about when you got in and out?"

"We got in from the point," Pep said. "No one can see that far out in the dark."

"They might from up high," I told him.

"And who would be watching the lake from above at this time of night?" he asked.

Oh no. I walked into more traps than a blind bear.

"Nobody." I tried not to sound suspicious, but Pep looked at me extra hard.

Mem started to smile like I'd just told her my teacher gave me the student-of-the-year award. "Suits or no suits. You . . ." she pointed at me, "were on the beach."

"Aye!" Pep said it like he'd just realized it himself. "She was. Our little girl was on the beach."

He rushed forward to hug me. "Way to go, lass."

I had been on the beach. Scared out of my head, but I was on the beach. Afraid for Mem and Pep, not me. I guess that meant I'd made some progress.

"Was that what you were up to last night?" Mem asked.

I waited, not ready to tell them. Not wanting to give them such a gift after they'd scared me so.

"Well?" Pep loosened his hold to let me dangle a little.

I chewed my lip, deciding.

Pep peered out of the corner of his eye at Mem, cocking his eyebrow. "Mem, I believe we have a girl who's been doing a bit of scheming."

How did he know about our silkie spotting plan?

"Really now?" Mem leaned into Pep's shoulder like she'd come in to have a closer look at a boo-boo on my arm.

"Well now, I figure her for taking a bit of a water step of her own." He pursed up his lips, saying, "What do you say to that, Kyna?"

I clenched my teeth, trying to hold it in, but I saw the look in their eyes, the *please* of it, the way Mem gripped Pep's shoulder, hoping. And I had to say it. "Yeah, I guess I tried."

"Whoo-hoo!" Mem shouted. "I prayed it be true. Thank you, Good Giver!"

Turning out of Pep's arms, I said, "It's not a big, big deal. It's not like I got in the water."

"And when was the last time you got that close to the water?" Pep asked, just as Mem held my arm up boxer-won-the-fight style.

A spark flew inside my head, setting off a memory. *I felt my arms raised up by helping hands, saw my feet plodding through wet sand, heard myself laugh as the waves tickled my feet.*

*Waves. Just waves. Cool. Wet. Not clawing and cold. Not dangerous or dark. Just cool. And wet. And those hands, holding mine. Wet, but holding fast.*

I snapped back to the moment, feeling all tickly inside and a bit scared.

My mind scrambled a bunch of ideas around, each of them hopping and jumping, fighting to get me to see something. Photographs flashed in my head like memories. Kenny skipping rocks on the beach . . . Grandma Bella holding up a tiny, tiny fish she'd caught . . . Mom and Dad dancing on a dock in swimsuits and flippers . . . photos, but not real memories. Faces I loved to stare at, not just because it made me feel close to them, but so my eyes didn't wander and see that ocean blue. Water. It stole so much from me. I couldn't even remember the times when those photos were taken because they revolved around water, just like the stories that Mem and Pep didn't want to tell me about from their childhoods. If I fought this fear, I'd get a lot more than wet. I might just remember my birth family. Feel my mom hold my hands. Maybe even learn a bit about Mem and Pep.

"What is it, love?" Mem asked.

"Just a memory of Mom." I tried to smile, but I wanted that moment I remembered back. To feel Mom again. To hear her laugh echo mine. And to know the feeling of water when I actually liked it.

Pep gave Mem a quick look, then slipped out of the room. When a memory of my mom came for a visit, I wanted Mem and only Mem. Well, really I wanted my mom. The mom who smelled of melon and wore pearls when she sailed. But it felt good to have Mem pull me into bed and hold me.

Mem pulled off my shoes, saying, "Care to tell me what you remembered?"

I shook my head, wanting to keep it safe and close.

Pulling my shirt off, a sleeve a time, Mem began to talk. At first, I didn't want to listen. I had a memory to hold onto, but then I heard the words she said and realized I had to listen.

"Me mem had eyes so brown and bright they almost looked like a bit of bronze in the sun. She loved a good cove at low tide in late afternoon. Finding herself a good spot, she'd just nestle down into the water like it weren't nothing more than a safe, warm bath. Then she'd watch the fish swim on by, loving how they moved like streamers through the water, looking the same, but each one different—a frilled fin there, a white scale here, a dot where no one else had it. Made her wish she could touch them, but if she so much as moved, they fled as if she meant to make a lunch out of them."

As that story settled over me like snow, I cried. To be close to my mom. To hold Mem's hand even tighter as she pulled the blanket over us. To finally meet my Grandma Monahan. Knowing all I needed to focus on in that memory was her face, the bright brown eyes and the happy smile. No water, just fish floating by with flipping fins, and happy gills.

"What was your mem's name?"

Mem turned my hand over in hers and tracked the lines in my palm, whispering, "Brida. And she sang me to sleep on many a night."

*Bree-dah.* It sounded like a word meant to be sung. And I could feel it like a musical note rising inside my head. I had me a new Gram. And two bright and happy memories to hold onto. If I fought hard, I'd get a flood of them, I felt sure. So I snuggled down with Mem and fell asleep to the sound of her singing an old Irish fishing song.

# MEMORY

Memories of my birth family had grown so old, they came out broken. The smell of cinnamon and flowery perfume made me see my grandma handing me a slice of toast. When I heard the tune of a jack-in-the-box, my brother hopped in a circle in my head, holding up one foot and calling out, "My toe! My toe!"

I usually only recalled wisps of my mother, a crinkle-eyed smile or a tickle-the-ear snatch of laughter. Until we came to the lake, I'd never remembered my mother and me together. Only three years old when she died, my memories were too frail and thin to last, but somehow I'd held onto that one of me and Mom going into the water together. I couldn't recall what beach or what the body of water was called.

Ah, the water. I remember enjoying the water, the cool wetness of it. The way it pushed against my ankles as I splashed through it. The pulling wetness had a sureness to it—a hugging kind of grip I liked. I liked it. I liked the water. I wanted to turn around, tell my mother. See her—know what she wore, how her face looked, but all I could conjure were my own feet. But I kept trying all day. Imagining that beach again and again until the water was nothing more than foamy static in my mind.

From my perch on the deck, I watched the sun let out its red parachute to set. I wondered just what other memories I could fish out of my mind. Spotting a puddle in the driveway, I walked over, waded in— reminding myself with just a little wet tug, a watery little hug.

Holding onto that memory of my feet in those friendly waves, I lowered myself down, feeling the cool muddiness of it like a wet blanket under me—it could fold over me, I thought.

No, no, it's just a little water. Not enough to drown a bug. So I lay there—wet and muddy, and tried to recall my own laughter.

Big deal. I'd flopped down in a puddle. Like I could drown in that. Flicking mud, I started to think about water and memories, and how just one drop held my whole life in a way. The love of this stuff drew my family out onto the waves day after day until it took their lives. Even tried to take mine.

I stood up feeling soggy and stupid, but as I caught sight of the sail-smooth water of the lake, the glossy sway of it pulled me in a little. Set me to thinking—water flowed through my life, reaching back to a shore I could no longer see. My family stood there—laughing, Mom and Dad with a cooler between them, Kenny racing on ahead, Gram with her slicker over her arm, headed for the boat they loved. And from that shore, the water ebbed back to me, to rocks among swirling waves, Mem and Pep standing there waving, calling me to join them.

I could live my life afraid of sinking to the bottom of those memories or I could learn to float. Carry myself to the memories I wanted to keep. Make even more among the waves with Mem and Pep. Yeah, I could, if I ever got brave enough to step foot in water again.

# STEPS

After calling into the house to let Mem and Pep know I was on my way to Tylo's, I headed down to the beach. Didn't even wait for them to answer me. Didn't want to give them time to realize I planned to take the beach route and have them make a big production out of it. I wasn't about to try going in the water, but I could plant my feet on the rocks and make my way to Tylo's. Why not? People did it every day. And today, I planned to do it without fear. No worries darting around me like spirits. I'd take my first real walk on the beach since I didn't know when, but I wanted the trip to be mine. Not ours.

Funny how my feet felt kind of light going down.

Didn't want to let go of the railing, but I went a little fast down those steps and onto the rocky beach. Kept the swing in my mind going to the rhythm of the waves. *Up, then back. Up, then back.* The crunchy sand under my shoes made me a little nervous. The shiftiness of it like the floor of a ride at the fair—it could tilt out from under me at any second. I wished beaches had hand rails.

The wind picked up a little. Heard the rustle of it in the leaves like chatty little rapids in a stream. No worries. The water didn't even reach me. I had plenty of beach. And a lot of nice, sturdy rocks to climb on. Told myself I could probably reach Tylo's if I went far enough. I crept along the beach, weaving behind the rocks. Keeping my eyes on dry land. Still felt the wind pushing at my back like one of those bratty kids who wants to be first to get a piece of the chocolate pudding pie the cafeteria ladies make once a month for birthday lunch.

A sudden coolness made me look up. Gray clouds made the sky look crabby. Where did they come from? The sky had been happy and blue when I stepped onto the deck just awhile ago.

I looked over my shoulder. I could go back. I'd get home before the clouds even thought of letting go of the rain. But that'd be giving in. Giving up.

No. I'd just hurry it up a bit and beat the rain. Fear wouldn't turn me around like a chime in the wind today. No, sir. I'd go my own way.

The wind had other ideas, whooshing in to pull off my hat. Saw it swept toward the water, but I jerked my head away before I could see it churned under. Hated that ratty old hat anyway.

More and more rocks cluttered the beach as I got closer to Tylo's. The wind picked up, lashing the trees until all their leaf rattling made them sound angry, too. A quick check told me the gray skies had started growing darker, the fear inside me getting just as ugly and black. The going got a little tougher with all the rocks, but I went faster. I could beat the storm. Outrun my fear.

The first thunderclap made me jump, daring me to look. To see what the coming storm had done to the water. I could hear it in the *chop, chop* of the waves as they slapped at the rocks, feel it in the wet gusts of wind against my face. My lungs had started to shrink, making it tough to get a full breath.

*No. Keep your course. Don't turn back.*

I stared at the shoreline above me, just trees and more trees. *Where did that stupid Tylo live, anyway?*

I started to run, tripping over rocks. Thunder boomed closer. Steps. I could see steps ahead.

Lightning cracked. Too close. I ran faster. But the clouds let out the rain before I'd made it three rocks farther down the beach. The water hit me like hot oil from a frying pan, burning a memory back into my body.

*Rain so thick I couldn't see beyond the wet, red shoulder I stared over, looking, searching for someone, the rain like a wrinkled shower curtain clouding my vision. Bouncing against that shoulder, the arms that gripped me tight didn't make me feel safe enough. Not in the wind that tore at the hat tied around my head. Not with the tilt of the boat toward the churning sea. I cried. Cried to be dry. Cried to be out of the storm. To be with my daddy. My daddy, who had run into that terrible rain to find Kenny. My brother, Kenny.*

*"We're almost there!" I heard my mother yell, then I turned to see the stairs lighted in the darkness ahead, the lantern hung above the door clanking against the wood. But a swell knocked everything loose, the lantern went flying, the deck lurched, Mom lost her balance, fell to the deck. Landing hard, her grip loosened and the wave crashing over the deck swept me away.*

I fought hard to get ahead of the memory, to push it back before I slid into that water, but the rain kept coming, my mind kept going deeper, falling into that night, so deep I couldn't crawl back out.

*Mom scrambled to catch me, the water spraying over her as I slapped at the wet deck for something to hold onto before I slid right off the edge. The fall into the water felt like I'd been swallowed into the storm itself—all wind and rain and anger twisting me around.*

*Then the water. The furious waves that chewed me up, pulling me down, not letting me go. I kicked, I screamed, I clawed, but the water just kept churning and churning, filling my mouth and my lungs, not letting me cough it out.*

Even on the beach of Lake Champlain where only rain threatened me as I clung to a boulder for safety, I choked on the memory of those waves.

*I wanted my mommy. Needed my daddy. Why didn't they help me? Why didn't they come? Too young to know they couldn't, I screamed for them, swallowing more water.*

*The waves washed over me. I came up sputtering, kicking and flailing, then I started sinking again. Down into the dark water that churned me around, filled me up until my chest near about exploded. Just as my mind gave in, something swept against my legs, then an arm closed around my waist and pulled me up. Then blackness.*

My mem said she held me to her as she swam sidestroke toward the shore. How did she find me in all that dark water? Carry me to the rocks against those angry waves?

*I woke to find her cradling me, patting out that water, trying to smooth out my terror with her warming hands, but I felt the tightness in her as she watched the waves, heard the prayers pouring from her lips. She prayed for Pep. Prayed he'd find my family. Return safe to her.*

*I screamed for my mom. Fought to get away so I could find her and Dad. But Mem held me fast until Pep pulled himself ashore, panting and pale like a fish pulled out of the water after a long struggle against the fishing line. But he could save no one but himself.*

As I hugged the rock on the lake's shore, the rain poured over me. I cried. Cried for my mom, my dad, Grandma Bella, and Kenny. Cried to have them there with me. As I looked out over the choppy waves, anger shook me from the inside out.

Grabbing a rock, I threw it in, wishing it could shatter that lake like glass. Tossing rock after rock, I screamed and yelled at that stupid, awful water for taking them from me. I wanted to see it hurt, but it only twisted and turned in the wind, coming again and again to the shore.

Angry, tired, and wet, my eyes fell upon a shell, eddied in, then out, in, then out, by the waves crashing in, then washing back out. They came day and night, again and again, never really changing except in speed and strength, shaped by the wind and the pull of the moon, but always coming back. The water didn't care. Didn't live like people do. Water would never change. I couldn't hurt it. Couldn't punish it for hurting me.

Only I could change. Grow stronger.

Standing, I walked away from that water to the stairs leading up to dry ground and a place where I could let go of all that anger. Let it sail out to sea and never return.

# CLAN

Funny thing I realized about lake houses as I walked along the upper edge of the shoreline—they have two fronts. Driving up to our lake house, I had seen all of the name plaques hanging from posts, mailboxes, and even trees. Each sign gave the family name of the people who lived at the end of the driveways we passed. As I read them, they almost seemed to be inviting us to come for a visit. Now that I walked on the shore side of the houses, I saw a whole new set of signs with the same names—Holbrook, Ryan, and Lushia—all silent wooden invites to come in from the rain. And a good thing, too, or how else would I have found Tylo's house in that storm?

Knocking on the door, I didn't expect to find a storm inside, but that's what I got. The door flew open with a bang as Tylo's mom rushed out to pull me inside, shouting, "Kyna! You're Kyna, right?"

"Yes," I said, as she started to dry me off with the towel she'd had over her shoulder, rubbing my head like I was the family dog caught in the rain.

She kept talking in a gust of words as two of her sons fought over one of those handheld game gadgets and another dive-bombed a row of marshmallows on the counter with baby potatoes. "Your parents are a mess trying to find you!"

"I told them I was coming here," I said, pulling my head free.

"Well, you must have been using a language only dogs can hear." She shook her head and started to take my shirt off.

"Hey," I grabbed my shirt.

"Oh," she looked embarrassed for only a second, then she shuffled me into the laundry room. "Sorry, dear. Used to having only boys."

Closing the door, she yanked off my shirt before I had any chance to even speak, telling me, "Your mother's calling all over the neighborhood, trying to find you. Your father's out on foot. My husband

132

even took Tylo out to search the woods."

She tugged and pulled and got me into dry clothes so fast I wondered if she'd roped and branded cattle in a past life. "Really, Tylo dragged his dad out to look for you. And here you are!" Stepping back, she took a look at me in the baggy shorts and too big T-shirt she'd dressed me in. Probably Trevor's.

"You don't look so frightened."

"I'm not." I laughed, so shocked to even say such a thing, let alone feel it.

"Well, good. I better call in the troops." She headed back into the kitchen.

Speaking into the walkie-talkie, she said, "We found her, Mr. Monahan. We found her."

Tylo answered back in a crackly shout, "This is me, Mom."

"Sorry." Mrs. Bishop grabbed another walkie-talkie on the counter. "Mr. Monahan?"

"Aye," Pep's worried voice came back.

"She's found her way to my house."

"Is she there, now?"

She handed me the walkie-talkie instead of answering. Felt kind of jittery to tell him, "I'm here, Pep."

"Silkies be praised, you're safe."

"Sorry I scared you. I thought you heard me say I was going to Tylo's."

"You stay put now. We'll sort that out later. Let me talk to Mrs. Bishop."

"Okay."

Pep had Mrs. Bishop call Mem and before I even had a chance to swallow the marshmallow Tylo's brother Greg offered me, people started flooding into their house. And flooding fit because everyone showed up soaking wet in a gust of wind and rain from the lake-side door, the front door, a side door—Tylo and his dad, Pep, Mem, Aunt Rosien, and even a whole crew of people I didn't know. They'd called out an army to find me.

And now that they'd found me, they planned to kill me. Tylo kept hitting me with his bag, yelling at me for running off. Pep scooped me up and hugged me so hard a rib nearly popped out of my mouth. Mem kept squeezing me, then stepping back to look me over, then squeezing me again. I started to get a little dizzy. Aunt Rosien said, "Like to kill her parents for the worry of it."

Everyone shouted and talked and carried on. Mrs. Bishop made tea and ordered her boys to make cocoa—three spills, a marshmallow fight, and a stern shout from Mr. Bishop later, we all sat in their living room talking, a fire roaring and the stones of the fireplace heating up. Well, the Bishop boys did a little more kicking and threatening than talking, but I didn't care. I sipped cocoa on a cushy couch with Mem and Pep sandwiching me, stopping to give me a kiss or a pat between sips of tea.

Everyone expected a big adventure story, but I just said that I'd walked along the beach and got caught in the rain. That's all that happened really. Or at least that's all I wanted to say in front of so many people I didn't know.

"Got any salt?" asked a man with spiky little gray hairs in his mop of brown.

Mrs. Bishop tried not to look surprised when the man sprinkled it in his tea and passed it down. Friends of Mem and Pep, no doubt. I began to wonder if everyone from Ireland had salt in their tea.

From their hand-knitted jumpers and their baggy pants, the men who'd come in with Pep looked like they'd dressed out of his closet, and the clanking cups with the *"slancha"* salutes said for sure that they came from Ireland like him. Mates of his, I'd bet on it. So, why haven't I ever met them?

The ladies who'd arrived with Aunt Rosien had the same wild hair look. Their linen shirts, long skirts, and rope sandals made me peg them as nature lovers like her.

The whole lot of them chatted all hunched over their cups, their voices pitching and rolling like waves. And when one of them called out a question, they all seemed to turn as one to answer.

They looked so out of place in a living room of DVDs, Nikes, and slogan T-shirts. As they all got to talking about the lady of the lake who wandered the shores calling out for lost children with their mile-a-minute Irish accents, I saw a likeness among them, like a clan had come to visit. Maybe they were commune folks living in the nature they fought to protect.

Leaning into Mem, I whispered, "Are these people nature hippies?"

Giving me a squeeze, she said, "In a manner of speaking, they are."

The thought of all those folks living together in the woods made me think it was a bit like a summer camp for adults that lasted all year. I started to laugh.

"That's a bit rude, love," Mem said, nudging me.

But why would so many folks from Ireland come to a lake in New York? I'd heard there are more Irish and their descendants in America than in the whole of Ireland, but why would such a loyal nature-loving lot come here?

Maybe it had something to do with that governor of Vermont who tried to have the lake declared a Great Lake so it would get the same conservation funds as the rest of them? They might have thought it wasn't getting the protection it needed. But I'm sure that could be said of plenty of lakes in Ireland.

I figured their reason for being there wasn't as important as the discovery that a small part of Ireland lived right there on the lake. Why hadn't Mem and Pep told me?

That would have made coming to the lake so much easier. If Mem and Pep wouldn't go back to Ireland because I was too afraid to fly over the ocean, then they could at least have a reunion with the folks they'd known back home. I would have jumped at the chance to spend the summer with people who knew them before I came along. Lake or no lake.

I'd heard my share of the banshee stories the lot of them were going on about, so I didn't feel bad about asking, "What were Mem and Pep like before they saved me?"

The whole lot of them started to speak with "well nows" and "you sure you want to hear about that rogue" and "my can I tell you a story" all in a bunch.

They had my heart racing for some real stories, but Pep popped off the couch, saying, "We'll save those tales for another night. We've overstayed our welcome with this kind Bishop family already. Heavens, it's like they've been invaded by the Green Brigade this evening."

With the nearly matching clothes and the way they moved almost like they knew each others' next move, I couldn't help but think that Mem and Pep's friends did look like a group of soldiers called out to rescue me. They could have been the Green Brigade—those Irish soldiers from the Civil War.

"Good night, Ian. Keep to the jet stream, Morigan. Blessing to you, Gavin." They all said their good-byes with kisses and well wishes like family. Had Mem and Pep lived in their commune? Were my parents real honest-to-goodness hippies?

Wading through the sea of folks in his front hall, Tylo grabbed my arm and handed me a walkie-talkie. "Take this. You ever get lost, you call in."

"Are you sure?"

"We have like a million sets. We could keep track of every raccoon in Clinton County if we wanted to."

"Thanks."

He blushed and started to sidestep and stare at his feet.

Leaning over to be heard amongst the good-byes and thank yous, I said, "Spotting tomorrow night?"

"You bet." He kind of hopped. "You still owe me some Irish barnacles."

"That's biscuits."

"Oh," he smiled. "Good, because even if they are cookies, I don't want to eat any barnacles."

"Good night."

"Night."

# GROUND

Mem and Pep herded me home. "Did you both live with those folks?" I asked as we left the lights of the Bishop house to enter the darkness of the woods.

"Never mind that." Mem gave my shoulder a tug. "What I want to know is what you were doing wandering off with a storm coming in?"

"I didn't see the storm. I just wanted to go to Tylo's. I called into the house to tell you I was going."

"Since when do you tell us where you're going rather than ask?" Pep wanted to know.

"I . . . I . . ."

"That's what I thought."

"But I did it. I walked on the beach."

"Don't think you can distract us, young lady." Mem tapped my head. "You can't go wandering off without permission."

"Yes, ma'am."

"Well, you just remember that each night next week when you have to bid Tylo happy hunting."

"No!"

"That's going light, if you ask me," Mem said. "I could use a bit of help cleaning that house of ours from top to bottom."

"No way!" When Mem said "clean," she meant sleeves up, knees down on the floor, scrub until you faint kind of clean.

"And I could use a little help organizing all my files and shelving all my books." Filing and alphabetizing until my eyes crossed? No, thank you.

Tugging at Pep's sleeve, I said, "Please no, please?"

"All right then, you should be happy with no owl hunting or leaving the house with Tylo for a week."

"And I can't believe I'm saying this," Mem shook her head, "but no going down to the lake either."

"Okay."

Funny, but I felt a little bigger, like I'd walked through the woods alone for the first time. I'd never been grounded before. Never left Mem and Pep long enough to get into any kind of trouble. I felt bad for worrying them. Knew I'd done the wrong thing by not asking them if I could go, but I still felt pretty good for heading out on my own and for not going stone freaky when that storm hit. Hey, I'd even faced down my worst memory and come out walking on my own two feet. Grounded or not, it felt pretty good to take a step in the right direction.

# STORIES

Tylo showed up for owling the next night. All I had to offer him were shortbread biscuits and milk. After a little pouting and a mouthful of biscuits, he seemed just fine with that.

"These cookies are great, Mrs. Monahan!" he said, doing the Cookie Monster spray with his crumbs.

Pep tapped him on the head with the daily paper as he passed. "I made them."

"You did?" Tylo asked, swigging milk. "My dad tried making rice cereal bars once and he thought if he cooked the marshmallows until they got black they'd be like burned campfire bars. Didn't work. We had to throw out the pan."

Pep laughed. Mem made a noise while washing the dishes—a warning Pep didn't listen to at all. "Itha there's grand at the cooking, but baking? Run out of the kitchen if you plan to live. That one used salt instead of sugar in making soda bread. Now, I like my water salty like any ocean-loving fella, but not my bread."

"You drink salt water?" Tylo asked.

Pep took a swig of his tea, "Doesn't everybody?"

Tylo stared at me. I recognized the look. The *are your parents for real?* stare I got any time I brought a new kid home. With all their talk of salt water, fairies, and silkies, who could tell what was real and what was joshing?

But Tylo didn't seem to mind. He just wiped his mouth with his sleeve, then sat forward to ask, "So how many silkies have you seen?"

Oh, no. Now he'd really find out how crazy my parents could be.

Pep tilted his head a little, like he might have water in his ear, then said, "Did you say, silkies?"

"Yeah, silkies. I've seen one. Heard more, but I just saw the one."

"Did you now?" Pep's smile looked forced, like he heard a joke he didn't like, but wanted to be polite.

I'd expected Pep to go into his now-let-me-tell-you-this-about-that storytelling mode. Why didn't he? Oh, right. He wasn't into telling any stories that day. I'd been trying since breakfast to get him and Mem to tell me more about the friends who'd helped them in their search for me, but I'd only gotten, "Oh, they're just old friends," over and over.

"That's right." Tylo pointed at me to tell them about our silkie spotting.

If Pep knew about that, he'd start thinking I believed his fairy tales, so I body-checked Tylo and said, "I told him you know the story of how the silkies got into this lake."

Tylo stared at me, but I'd found Pep's on switch. He got all chipper and set to telling, "Oh, of course I do. Every good Irish lad knows how the silkies came to Lake Champlain."

And off he went. I sat there listening, knowing the words so well they just flowed through my head like music.

Why couldn't Pep talk to me like that about the real past? About his own family? Mem had at least told me about Brida and her brother Shannon. But Pep hadn't told me a thing about his childhood. Yet, I knew fairies stole children, pookas preyed on lost travelers, and brownies would never touch a shoe. I knew more about a bunch of mythical creatures than I did about my own dad.

"Did you hear that, Kyna!" Tylo gave me a shove. "There's a whole pod of them in the lake. We're bound to get a picture of one. You'll win that ribbon for sure!"

Great. Now my parents were going to think I really believed in silkies. I'd never hear the end of it. But they just stared at me, Mem standing beside Pep, her hand on his shoulder.

Mem sounded distracted, even distant. "How about a board game?"

"Oh, right," Tylo shook his head. "You're grounded."

"Doesn't mean we can't have fun here." Mem forced a smile, then led the way into the living room. We may have taken over Atlantic City in Monopoly and become a human pretzel in Twister, but Mem and Pep seemed to be pushing themselves to have fun. I kept wondering what had happened. Did they finally see something wrong with all their silly fairy tales now that a friend of mine believed in them?

After Tylo went home, full of biscuits and goofy stories to tell his brothers, I said to them, "You know I don't really believe in silkies. I just told Tylo I did so we could be friends."

Mem glared at me. "Kyna Moira Monahan, what kind of friendship can be built on a lie?"

"Just a little one. He had to have seen something in that lake. I'll just take a picture of it and prove to him that it isn't a silkie."

"You'll do no such thing. You're grounded, remember." Mem spoke to me in anger, real face-twisting anger. I'd never actually seen her mad like that before.

"Okay." I felt like shrinking into my slippers and shuffling off to bed.

Pep didn't even try to lighten things up with a joke. He just kept putting the games away.

"I'm sorry."

"You should've thought of that before you ran off and tangled the Bishops up in this mess."

"Itha," Pep breathed out a warning as he stood.

Mess? What mess? I'd just said I would take a picture of a silkie.

Mem stomped off, spurting something in Irish. Pep followed her, answering in the same language. I hated it when they did that.

As I tromped off to bed, my thoughts started bumping around, trying to figure things out. What had Mem and Pep so out of sorts? Pep seemed awful nervous when I had tried to ask questions of his friends. Is that what started things in the wrong direction?

I could see all those people in my mind. How they sat so close together, wore such similar clothing, and turned as one when someone spoke. They reminded me of something I'd seen—bright, fluid, moving as one, like . . . like a school of fish. The fish Grandma Brida used to love to watch. That set me to wondering. How'd she just sit there and watch fish underwater?

Mem's description of her childhood echoed in my ears, "Most days you couldn't catch me out of the water."

And all the sea animals she'd saved. And me. She'd saved me. Pep tried so hard to save my family he nearly died. Practically living in water, saving people, born in Ireland . . .

No. They couldn't be. Silkies aren't real. They're make-believe. Silkies didn't live in that lake or come onto dry land to hide their pelts and walk around like regular people. If they had, Mem and Pep would've died of sadness long ago.

I mean, they'd been away from the water for a good eight years now. How could they live that long out of the water? That question sat me up in bed. Was that why they'd come back to Lake Champlain? To be with other silkies? To swim at night as seals, then return to the house as humans in the light of day?

My parents couldn't be silkies. That'd be like finding out your grandfather was Santa Claus. But the salt in the tea, the silence about their past, the love of water, the protection of nature, it all fit.

But if it fit, I didn't. I'd kept them away from water. Made them live in a dry, dusty old house miles and miles and miles away from the ocean or even a lake. Was that why they wanted me to get over my fear of water so they could tell me their secret? Return to the sea?

Would they find me new parents and leave me here?

I wanted to cry out. To bring them running so they could hold me and tell me it would all be okay.

"No silkies here," Pep would say.

"Just us Irish," Mem would laugh.

That's right. I'd let my imagination run away with me. Mem and Pep just loved the water like I loved photography and walks in the woods, and I'd get that photograph of a dog or a jumping fish or whatever Tylo had seen in the water and prove it once and for all. There are no silkies. And my parents are just as normal and everyday as the bed in which I tried to sleep.

But every time I shut my eyes, I could see Mem and Pep far out on the rocks, looking back at me over their shoulders just before they dove into the water and swam and swam, far away from me.

# PAST

I woke up to find Pep perched on my windowsill, his feet in the chair next to it. He sat there writing fast and furious, like it might save a life. Seeing me awake, he said, "Now before you set your mind to thinking, answer me this. What would've happened if Mem and I didn't let you go taking those water steps? Just threw you in a lake to make you learn to swim again?"

The very idea had me scrambling against the wall, pulling the covers up against me, ready to kick and scream until he forgot any such notion.

Pep dropped his notebook and jumped to his feet. "Hold on, now." He looked frustrated, scared even. He cursed in Irish, I could hear the bite of it in the words. "I'd never do that, Kyna. You know that."

Catching my breath, I nodded, agreeing. Sure, Mem and Pep pushed me to get over my fear, but hadn't they given me seven long years to do it?

Yeah, they did.

And if what I'd thought the night before could be, might be true, why would they leave me now if they'd already stayed all this time? Had I taken too long to overcome my fear? Did they have to return to the water or . . . I didn't even want to think it. Not Mem and Pep. I loved them so much.

The idea of it had me stunned. I just sat there, listening, struggling to pull in the fear that came spilling out of me.

Pep said, "You see, Kyna, a pep tries to do the right thing. But it's hard. You don't always know what that is."

I wrestled with the very same problem. It made me shiver from the inside. Did I tell them I'd figured out they were silkies? Would they laugh at me?

Pep said, "And with the story behind where your mem and I come from, well, telling you that story would be a bit like dropping you into a lake. A little too much all at once. Thought we could do it a bit at a time. In steps, like we've done with water."

Fairy steps? Was that why Pep had been telling me all those stories about fairies and pookas and leprechauns? He wanted to get me to make room in my mind for the idea that such creatures could be real? To believe that he and Mem were actually silkies?

To find out if that'd been his plan, all I had to do was say it out loud. *Silkies. You and Mem are silkies.* Just a few little words. Why couldn't I get them to come out of my mouth?

Because I didn't want them to be true. Didn't want to know they'd lived all cooped up and dry so far away from their families and their watery home just because I couldn't face my stupid fear.

But no more. I'd do it. I'd face that water and win. Then they could tell me. I could watch them dive into that water and not be scared. Not worry that they'd drown or swim away from me.

But just the thought of them standing on those rocks, looking over their shoulders, then diving into that deep, dark water where I couldn't go had me ready to curl up into a ball like a poked crab.

Angry at myself for letting fear pull me back again, I stood up, saying, "Maybe you should've just thrown me in. Made me face my fear and get it over and done with."

Pep's eyes went wide. "Well, I, for one, am not

ready to try that." He stood up. "Kyna, if we do the wrong thing here, your fear of water may have a hold on you for the rest of your life."

Not if I could help it.

"We all right with taking a few more steps then?" He looked down at me, hopeful.

I nodded.

"Right, then." He looked happy enough to float. "I'll set to fixing breakfast."

Giving me a kiss on top of the head, he walked to the stairs.

I went to my closet to get dressed, but my mind tossed and turned over the very idea that more than just the ocean stood between Mem and Pep and me. All this time, I'd thought they were Irish and I was American. Now they might be silkies and me only human. It's one thing to be a different nationality, but a whole different species?

"You trying your hand at mind control?" Mem asked, walking past my open door as she wrapped her wet hair into a towel. "The door opens much faster with the handle, see." She disappeared into her bedroom.

She seemed so normal. So Mem. How could she be a seal?

I stood there, staring at her closed door, trying to

fit my mind around the idea that Mem could slip into a seal's coat like it was nothing but a swimsuit, then dive into the water and *poof*, she had fins and whiskers and a walloping big tail.

"Trying my door, now are you?" Mem asked, coming back out in her day clothes. "Well, I'll leave it a bit open to give you more of a chance."

She smiled, but I could see her glimpse over her shoulder at me as she headed down the stairs. I saw a hint of worry in her eyes. A bit of the sadness I saw when she looked at me from those rocks, right before she dove into the water in my vision the night before.

That put me in motion, pushed me to find some clothes and face that stupid lake. I'd win this time. I'd walk right in without fear.

Had only one arm in my shirt by the time I realized I'd gone into staring and amazed mode again. I must have looked like I'd been stuck in pause there for a second. Back in play mode now, I realized that my closet had a map of the world printed over and over down the wall. I ran my hand over that map seeing all that water and realizing Mem and Pep could swim through seas, one after the other, saving lost ships, rather than being stuck here with me.

Drawing my hand over the ocean depth ripples drawn in the Atlantic Ocean, my mind fluttered, and my eyes saw other maps flipped down in front of me. The fluttering steadied and I saw a hand over a map, tracing an ocean route. I squinted to see the land mass nearby, trying to focus my memory.

Was it a memory or just a daydream?

*I could hear a low, excited voice talking as the hand tapped and pointed. I felt warm and rocked like someone held me in their lap. I couldn't make out any words on the map, just squiggles and lines, like I could only see them with the eyes of a small child.*

Slamming the door shut, I tried to block out the memory, knowing in that moment that I saw my father tracing our route out to sea off the coast of Maine. I wouldn't let him take me into a memory that scared me. Mem and Pep said Dad had charted a course to Nova Scotia. *"Maybe even Greenland,"* he'd shouted, laughing, *rocking back in his chair. I remember seeing him from behind, the chair leaning way back, him looking as if he might fall.*

*"Oh, Graham,"* Mom cooed. *I could hear her voice over my head, feel it vibrating behind me. Mom held me. I closed my arms over my chest to feel her hold me tight.*

Dad had stood up and left the room, his answer just a sound now that the memory had been worn thin like an old audio tape that had been played until the sound disappeared.

But I remember part of what Mom said next. *She turned me around, but all I could see were those pearls she wore as she said, "Now, Kyna, promise me this . . ."*

Promise you what, Mom? I strained to hear the rest, to pull it out of the murky depths of my memory, but nothing came. It all faded like the morning fog in the sun. No Mom, no pearls, no promise.

Maybe if I could remember more, pull myself back to the time when water didn't scare me, then I could not only retrieve the memories of my mother that I had lost, but I could drown my fears once and for all.

I went under my bed to pull out my memory box. As big as the suitcase I took to sleepovers, it held a photo album, the jack-in-the-box Kenny stubbed his toe on, Grandma Bella's recipe book with the chocolate stain on the cover, Dad's pipe, a rosy silk scarf I think belonged to Mom, and my little gumball orange slicker that I'd worn that day. I loved to hold it, crinkle its fabric and know that it was probably one of the last things my mom ever touched.

When I held it, I could almost feel her. I sat at the window, rocking, listening to the waves *swing in, swing out*, praying I could remember that time on the beach when mom held my hands as I played in the water.

Splashing. I could hear splashing. Had Pep gone to the beach? Or did that echo from my mind?

*I saw ripples of foam, felt it tickling my feet.*

*"Wave spit," Kenny called it, shouting as he ran. Ran down the beach, dragging a stick behind him. I tried to run too. But someone held my hands.*

*Mom.* I squeezed my hands to hold her there.

*Whoosh, she picked me up and swung me over the foamy waves, then dropped me splush into the water. No fear, just fun. Cool wet water up to my shins like I'd stepped into blueberry bug juice. I stomped. I splashed. The water sprayed a laughing woman. The woman who walked me into the water. My mother. My laughing mother bringing me into the water to play. And I loved it like I loved her. Splashing, dancing, hugging, kissing.*

I blinked. She disappeared. I sat on my bedroom floor, feeling her skin against mine. Hearing her laugh in my ears.

For a fleeting second, I actually wanted to go into the water. To follow that memory right into a wave. But the wave crashed over my head, the storm of a darker memory looming. I crushed my eyes shut to hold it back and imagined my mom laughing, slapping the water to invite me in. I'm coming, Mom. I'm coming.

# PROMISE

The promise my mom asked me to make all those years ago had been swallowed up by time. Did she want me to promise not to be as foolish and daring as my father, who tried to sail too far? Or was she asking me to be brave? To never fear the things that made her worry? Which is better? To be fearless and go too far? Or to never go at all?

Maybe both. Shrink the fear down to the right size. Don't let it disappear and lead you into foolishness, but don't let it get so big it drowns you. Pep had always told me that. So, I chose the promise to make to my mom. I'd never let fear run my life again.

I'd face it and let Mem and Pep know I had figured

out their secret. To lift the worry off their shoulders, I'd take a big water step all on my own.

I waited until Mem and Pep went for a swim, then I went to the last room in the house they'd expect to find me—the bathroom. Not for a sponge bath or a wimpy shower, but a sit-in-the-tub-filled-to-the-rim bath. After all, it's a "bath" room. And it was about time I proved once and for all water wouldn't kill me, not if I shrunk my fear down to the right size.

Pep had it right, jumping in the lake would be too big of a step, but a bath, that would do the trick. Didn't own a swimsuit, so I wore a pair of shorts and a T-shirt, got in the tub and sat down to settle myself. I shook inside and out. Gripping the edge of the tub, I said, "*Just a little wetness. A little cool cleanness.*" I could hear Pep in my head, talking me through it like he had when I took my first shower.

Closing my eyes, I pulled my feet back and turned the water on. Hot. Cold. It didn't matter, that water stung. Made me cry. But I planted myself in that tub, held my breath and let that stupid, clinging, snaking, ugly water wash around me. Then I stuffed that plug in and let it rise.

To my knee. I let out my breath. My thigh. I started to pant. My waist, each inch making it harder and harder to breathe. When my breathing turned to the stuttering of chills, I cranked off the water. I couldn't look at it, not with the way the movement made it swish from side to side, pulling at me like waves. Waves that could pull you under and choke you.

I grabbed the sides, ready to bolt, then wrestled myself back down.

*You are going to stay in this tub, Kyna Moira.*

*Just a little wetness.*

I put my hand down to the bottom of the tub. Eyes closed, I scooped up a little water and let it trickle down my arm from the shoulder. I'd seen kids do that at the pool to get used to the coldness of the water before they dove in. Just the idea had me shaking my head, repelling imagined water from dry hair.

*A tub, Kyna. You're in a tub. To get away, all you'd have to do is stand up. Don't panic, just hold the sides, put your legs out, and lean back like it's nothing more than a lawn chair.*

*Yeah, right. A lawn chair that could kill me.*

*It's just a tub.*

I gripped the sides. My legs squeaked against the porcelain as I straightened them out. Easing back, my muscles locked up. I felt like a rusted chair myself, fighting to loosen up enough to lower into the water.

My shoulders ached. My jaw twitched. I could feel the coldness on my back. The water touched me, feeling slimy. Just a little bit farther. It pulled at my shirt. Wet my shoulder blades. It slicked the back of my head. Filled my ears.

*No. Not inside me.*

I tried to pull up, but my hand slipped. I flipped to the side, falling back into the tub, water splashing over my face, into my mouth, my eyes, my nose. Panic exploded inside me. I flailed, kicking, screaming, scrambling to get out.

The water fought back, choking me, stinging my eyes, blurring my vision. I struck my head against the side of the tub. Stunned, I slumped over, face first in the water. And that woke me up, sent me bolt upright, tossing my head back to shed that choking awful water.

Scrambling over the edge of the tub, I flung myself onto the rug and pulled it around me as I cried. Cried in fear. For being so small in the face of my fears. So much for my promise.

# SKINNY DIPPERS

So Mem and Pep wouldn't find me curled up like a beached baby whale, I scurried into my room and dried off with my blanket, then bundled up in as many warm clothes as I could find.

To keep my mind off what a fool I'd been, I tried to read a book, but I just kept going over the same sentence again and again, the words nothing but squiggly little lines like the names on that map my father traced.

Closing my eyes to clear my thoughts, I heard a staticky pop, then a voice shouting, "Kyna, Kyna, are you awake?"

Tylo? How could he be talking into my bedroom? Oh, the walkie-talkie he gave me. I dug under my dirty clothes to find it.

"Hello?" I shouted into the thing.

His voice came back. "I saw one. And it'll still be down there if you hurry."

Did I want to see it? Know for sure? Or better yet, should I let Tylo see it? Was that why Mem got so mad when she found out Tylo meant to take a picture of one? She didn't want anyone to have proof of the silkies in the lake.

"Come on!" Tylo shouted. "I heard it bark, then I saw it, swimming in the water as slick as you please."

There's nothing slick about swimming. "It was probably just a dog," I shouted to throw him off. "Besides, I'm grounded. Why don't you just come to my house. We can camp-out by the fire, make s'mores."

"No way. I'm not losing another chance to catch a silkie on film. I just need one picture. You can sneak out and be back before they know it."

I was afraid of what he'd know by the end of the night if I let him go.

"I don't think I can." I couldn't. Couldn't believe my parents might be mythical creatures. Or risk letting Tylo find out they really were.

Tylo called back, "I need this picture. People have to believe me. If I don't prove it, my brother Greg is going to keep putting diapers in my bag. And Trevor put a bottle by my plate at lunch. Do you know what they will be like once we get back in school? They'll tell everyone."

I knew exactly what it would be like. My little apple-bobbing freak-out gave the kids in fourth grade enough ammunition to tease me for a whole year, covering my notebook in little life jackets, offering me a rope to pull me back out when I went into the bathroom, calling me "water baby" for an entire year.

I couldn't allow something like that to happen to Tylo. He already had to live with his three evil brothers—being teased by the kids at school would be too much. For a friend like Tylo who'd searched the woods for me in the rain, I had to do something. But what?

"Okay, I'll go." I said, hoping I could figure something out before I reached the beach.

"Yippee skippee!" he yelled. "I'll meet you at the bottom of the steps by your place."

If I got back before Mem and Pep returned from their swim, they'd never know I left.

Just in case I didn't beat them home, I left a note for Mem and Pep on my pillow that said, "I'm with Tylo." Then I wrote, "I'm sorry" down the rest of the page.

To my surprise, the only thing that bothered me as I ran down the lakeside steps was the problem of finding a way to stop Tylo. Mem and Pep had been right again. Living on a lake had taken me one step closer to beating my fear of water. Half of me felt proud for getting so close, the other half wanted to run home.

"What took you so long?" Tylo asked when I reached the bottom.

"Had to leave a note."

"You haven't snuck out much, have you?"

"Nope."

"Stick with me," he laughed as we headed down the beach. "I've been trained for it."

I certainly wasn't trained for this. How could I turn him around? Maybe I could take a picture of a rock, a shadowy something he could tell his brothers might be a seal. But his brothers wouldn't believe him and Tylo might see too much. I was just about to tell Tylo we should turn back, when we heard it. A far off bark at sea.

"I hear them!" he shouted, grabbing my hand. "Let's go!"

He started to run, dragging me along behind him. I'd never even tried to move that fast on sand before, so I had all I could do to stay on my feet. I had heard it, though. A distant bark that echoed on the water.

That had my insides on spin cycle. That sound meant one thing to me. My parents had tails.

Tylo stopped dead. I slammed into him. "We've got to creep from here. They love this cove."

Too stunned to even think, I inched my way over the rocks, grabbing at Tylo when I started to wobble. Could I pretend to slip and drop my camera? It'd kill me to break it, but I had to do something.

"Shh," Tylo warned. "Listen."

We stopped mid-wobble and listened. Laughter, far out, then *splash, fwap* like a fin on water.

"That's them," he said.

Looking out at the rocky point, I froze, and not just because the rock I stood on started to tilt like the deck of a sinking ship. No, I recognized that point.

Mem and Pep had stood just there to wave at me the night I couldn't find them right away. The very point they stood on in my dreams just before they dove in and swam away forever.

Seeing it froze me to the spot.

"Let's go find them!" he shouted, running off.

"Tylo!" I grabbed for his collar, but went tipping toward the beach as he scrambled onto the rocks.

I regained my balance, then ran after him, thinking, *Oh, please let him see nothing but bobbing heads. Please.*

Climbing a rock, Tylo stood up and stared. "Oh whoa-whoa-whoa. No way."

He whispered, not the *look what I see* kind of whisper, but a *you can't believe this beautiful church* kind of whisper. "There's so many of them."

No way. Mem and Pep had spent their whole life protecting me and in one night I'd revealed their big secret. I climbed the rock, hoping I could turn things around—Tylo and all his ideas about silkies. But how?

As I stood on the shoulder-high rock, staring at that cove and the piles of clothes along the point like linen lichen, I sighed with relief. I had a way out of this one.

Tylo started hitting me. "Take a picture. Take a picture."

"Of clothes?"

"It proves it." Tylo hit me again. "They're silkies."

"No, they're not. They're hippies."

"Hippies?" Tylo stared at me, looking surly.

"Yeah, commune-living, nature-loving, swim-with-no-clothes-on hippies!"

"No way."

"Yes way."

I expected him to be grossed out and ready to go home.

But not Tylo. No, he said, "This I've got to see!" Then he ran off down the point before I could stop him. So much for my great cover-up.

# SHOTS

"Hippies?" Tylo stopped. He stared at the clothes. "Those aren't hippies," he panted, "they're the people from my house. Look—the same skirts and sweaters!"

I could see my hippie story dissolving faster than salt in tea.

Tylo spun to face me, "They are silkies! They're Irish. They love the water." He started hopping up and down and pointing, "So are your parents!"

Jeez, he's met them what, twice, and he already knows. Took me seven years. What a genius.

"Let's go back." I grabbed Tylo and gave him a tug. If I couldn't trick him into going home, maybe I could pull him.

"No way. I'm going out on the point to take a picture." He yanked the camera off my neck and started running.

I couldn't let him take a picture. My parents would be front page news on every weirdo newspaper in the country. That's what I got for wishing our family's picture could be front page news.

Waves or no waves, all I could see was Tylo's back as he ran down the point, my camera knocking against his side.

"Wait," I yelled.

Reaching the last flat rock, he slid to a stop, me slamming into him. "Shh!" He fumbled to get his binoculars. He scanned the horizon. I prayed he'd find nothing.

"Where are they?" He scanned again. "They have to be here. Look at those clouds." He pointed toward Vermont. Dark clouds hung over the lake like steel wool.

A storm. Those clouds woke me up. I stood on rock. Not a rock on a beach, but a stone dropped in the water, surrounded by waves. Tide-crazy, wind-frenzied waves, with a storm lurking. My lungs locked up. My joints filled with lead. I couldn't breathe. I couldn't move. I just wanted to scream.

"They've got to see the boats to safety."

Safety. I needed safety. Dry land.

"Wait, I see one." He backtracked toward the shore to get a better look, with me rushing along behind him. I could hear Tylo, but I didn't care what he said. I just wanted off those rocks and back in my bed. My safe bed.

"Another." He said, shuffling sideways, craning to look. Made me nauseous just to see him teetering so close to the water, but he kept right on talking. "They say silkies swim in pairs. Mates for life. Like wolves." He turned to face me, saying, "Want to see?" But seeing me, he said, "Are you okay?"

"I . . . I . . ."

"You don't look right. Are you going to hurl?"

Hurl! *No, don't hurl me in the water!* I grabbed Tylo's arm so he couldn't push me.

"Chill," he laughed. "We're safe with so many silkies here. They'll save you. And I need that picture." He pulled forward, dragging me. Even with me gripping for dear life, he got the camera to his face, then started searching the waves.

I closed my eyes, ready to cry. I couldn't look. Couldn't imagine what those waves would do if I fell in. But Mem and Pep. I had to protect them.

*Ca-ree, ca-ree.* A squeaky melodic call went out over the waves from the west.

"Hear that? They're calling to each other."

*Ca-ree, car-ee.* This time from the east. Such a sound. So clear. It drifted into me, comforted me. *Ca-ree. Car-ee.*

"Wish I could call back and lure them closer."

Felt the desire of it in my chest, the longing to call back.

Click. Tylo took the shot. "Got one!"

The longing grew, stretching down my arms, into my hands. I had to see them. Touch them if only with my eyes. I took the camera, used it like a set of binoculars to search the waves. Nothing more than water, dipping and swooning. Nothing more than waves.

*Ca-ree, ca-ree.* A brown head crested the water, a seal, then another. Click. Click. Two more farther out. Click. They patrolled. Swimming. Searching for anyone who needed them.

"We've got their pictures!" Tylo shouted, running ahead. "We'll be famous!"

He jumped in the air, but slipped as he came down, his foot going out from under him, his body pitching forward.

"Tylo!"

He fell so fast, he couldn't catch himself. He hit ear-first on the rocks, sliding toward the water. No. Not the water.

His arms didn't go out as he slid into the waves. He'd been knocked out. Unable to save himself even in shallow water.

I had to go in. Had to save him. But I couldn't move, the fear of it pressing me thin, drilling me into that rock. I felt the water that swallowed him filling my own lungs.

Then, in the call of a seal, I heard Pep say, *"You can't let your fears grow bigger than you, Kyna. They'll swallow you up."*

Just as the waves swallowed Tylo.

# RESCUE

I threw myself in. The water broke like glass over my skin. Only darkness surrounded me as I spun and fought to find Tylo. Weeds and rocks and eye-stinging water, nose-biting, lung-filling water. *Don't panic. It'll drown us both.*

I could do this. See what I wanted. Do what I wanted. Fear would not make me leave my friend. I promise, Mom. I promise.

Kicking, I thrashed through the water, my hands out, my eyes searching. Only dark and darker showed up in that water. No light reached a black-hole dark spot just a few feet ahead. I kicked again, pulling with my hands, then dove. Wet cloth. A boot. Tylo. I pulled.

I yanked. I pushed off the bottom with my feet and dragged him up and inland at the same time.

Breaking the surface of the water, I screamed for air. A need that stretched all the way back to that cold night when the sea took my family. I needed that breath to break free of my fears.

Pulling Tylo's face out of the water, I dug my heels in to backpedal to shore, yelling for him, "Wake up! Wake up!"

Dropping him on the beach, he fell like so much wet laundry. Taking CPR and first aid lessons like some kids learned to swim, I dropped to my knees and set to work. *Check for response.* "Tylo! Tylo!" *Open the airway. Give rescue breaths. Pump and blow. Pump and blow.*

He coughed. Forcing out the water. I turned him on his side to rescue position as he gasped for air.

Catching my own breath, I realized I'd started to cry. I sat on the beach. Wet to the bone. Staring at the water.

Eyes stared back at me.

Black, blinking eyes surrounded by gray hair, the smiling teeth so white, the chin just beneath the water. I knew those eyes. That gray, gray hair, like a mare in the meadow. Mem? Bobbing behind her, a larger face, eyes that made me feel safe. Could it be

Pep? Two more faces, then six. All of them watching. All of them waiting.

Tylo coughed, then sat himself up as I stared like I'd been frozen in place. "Wha . . . What happened?" He shook his head, then turned to face the same way I did and came nearly face to face with the whole pod. The whole clan of Terin. Or his descendants anyway.

Mem laughed, then tilted her head back to call out, *"Ca-ree!"* Her family answered, turning once again to sea. As they swam out, I saw the bottom of their feet come out of the water, once, twice, then fins. Tails splashing out of the water.

Who needed pelts? They just dissolved into their silkie selves right there in the water.

I ran. Ran right over those rocks.

Tired, Tylo called out, "I'll wait here!"

Ran through the thoughts. Realized things running from rock to rock. Mem and Pep had rescued me. Not from a cave on the shore, but the ocean. Silkies come to rescue the fools who've stayed out too long in a storm. They'd come to dry land for me. Raised me on two feet, leaving their pelts and their seal lives behind. Only knowing the freedom of the water when they could get away and swim in pools and waters polluted with chemicals. They'd done this for me. For me. Given up half their lives to make me feel safe.

Reaching the end of the point, I jumped down onto the rocks and put my hand out in the water. From the grayness of her pelt, I knew Mem swam to me first. I stroked her back, as smooth and gray as her long hair. I laughed. Pep came too, doing tricks, arching up in the water to swim backward, clap his fins, and bark. His brown hair looked almost red in the moonlight.

Silkies. My parents were silkies.

I stood up and did what any good daughter would do. I stepped in.

# LAST STEP

Not that I'd wish a concussion on any friend, especially not one as good as Tylo, but with his blurry vision and swimmy memory, I could convince him that we'd only seen an old sail rumpled on the rocks and my Aunt Rosien's pet seals at play. With my camera rock-smashed and waterlogged, he had no picture to prove me wrong.

As we trudged through the underbrush with my new camera in tow and a plan to photograph something on dry land like an owl, he said, "Hey, at least I really saw seals."

"Not everybody sees that on their summer vacation," I said, leading the way up into my tree house, a good roost for owl watching at dusk when they first come out.

"Yeah. Think you can win at the fair with this picture?" Tylo asked, pouring a cup of cocoa from his thermos.

"If we catch one in flight before winter." We'd been up there three nights in a row with no luck.

"And we're out of marshmallows."

"Greg?"

"You guessed it."

Guessed it. I would have never guessed that the whole reason Mem and Pep had dragged me all the way up to Lake Champlain was to reveal their big secret. Get me to finally face my fear of water so they could tell me the truth. The whole truth. And sometimes when I thought about Mem and Pep as shape-shifters who could go from being as human as me to seals as barky and spry as the ones I saw on the field trip to the zoo, the idea of it got so big I felt like floating. Some people find out their grandparents used to be hippies and got arrested for protesting, or that their mother once entered a beauty contest and wore a bikini in front of the whole town. Real mind-benders that make you see your family in a whole new way. But finding out your parents are mythical creatures, well, that one sets your mind on spin.

Had me so distracted, Tylo had to tap me with his cocoa cup and point when an owl set down in the high branches of a tree about a hundred feet away.

Put that camera his parents bought me for saving their son right up to my eye, complete with a zoom lens Pep paid for because I'd taken my biggest water step ever. As I watched that owl, its lantern eyes scanning for mice, I started remembering Mem's tale of the owl bride, a poor girl trapped in an owl's body by an evil witch, and it set me to wondering just how many of Mem and Pep's fairy stories had been real. Were fairies really pony-riding, baby-stealing little fiends?

The idea of it nearly turned me away from that owl, but when it screeched, Tylo took in a howl of a breath and I snapped shot after shot—those wings spreading out into the air like a glider launching from a cliff. *Snap. Snap.* I caught it tilting toward us, mid-dive. Could see the photo in my mind's eye . . . wings out, one tipped up, one down, wide-open eyes lantern yellow, talons down, ready to snatch up the mouse from the ground and fly away with it.

"You got it! You got it!" Tylo shouted, hitting me in the arm and tossing cocoa all over us both.

I sure did. I got a photo that could earn me a blue ribbon. And I finally understood all of Mem and Pep's stories and *you'll see when you're ready* secrets. And boy, did I feel ready. Giving Tylo a "catch you later," I raced down the ladder.

"Later, Water Girl!" he shouted from above.

Yeah, that's me. Water Girl. Miss Fear herself had actually rescued someone at sea. Well, at cove really. Where Tylo went in, he could've waded back out if he'd been awake.

I'd saved Tylo's life like Mem and Pep had saved mine. A little bit of silkie may have rubbed off on me over the years. But I doubted I could ever give up as much as they did for me. All I had to get rid of was my fear. And I nearly flew home without the weight of it on me. Even went by the beach route to get there.

Happy to know taking that one last water step brought me an ocean's worth of wonderful things. I'd saved my friend Tylo, faced my biggest fear, and found my families there. Not just the truth about Mem and Pep, but my birth family, too. Now I could think about them, pull back wisps of memory with no fear of the bad memories that lurked below. I could just splash and play with them, just like I did back then.

They say most of the world is water, so I guess that little belly flop into the lake opened the rest of the world up for me. And it felt good to wade around in it. Had me excited to see what Mem and Pep might be up to back at our place. Yes, it's ours now. We plan to stay all year, every year. And I'm just fine with that. They talked the Kenricks into selling them the cabin—apparently a broken leg while waterskiing was enough to turn Mrs. Kenrick off lake living. I certainly won't be trying waterskiing anytime soon, but I actually felt pretty good about living on the lake. We'll keep Grandma Bella's house for holidays. And Mem says I might want it for my own family someday.

I'll miss Hillary, but we'll keep in touch by sending each other photos. The first one I sent her is of me waving from the water. She's going to go into orbit over that one. I told her to show it to Bobby Clarkson.

Found Mem and Pep circling the dock. People style. With it just dark, they didn't dare go silkie when people could still see them.

"Skinny dipping," Pep laughed, taking another lap in his blue moon trunks.

They'd dragged the dock in, so I could get on it from a bridge. I lay down to look into the water over my folded hands.

"Did you fancy our birthday suits?" Mem said, turning on her back. Leave it to a silkie to be able to go that fast on her back, even with her legs.

"Pep's fur is red!"

"I guess it works like a beard. Some fellas with brown hair grow red beards. I guess red silkies can have brown hair."

"Fancy that." I sat up and crossed my legs. "So, are fairies really mean?" I teased.

"Next summer, we can take you to Ireland. And you can find out."

"Yeah, right. You're not even from Ireland."

"Am too." Pep straightened up to tread water beneath me. He made it seem as easy as breathing. For him it probably was. "It's your mother who's the Irish-American. We did meet in Ireland like we said. She wanted to see the Mother Sea. Can't say as I blame her. At least we've got salt."

Mem splashed him good.

So Mem and Aunt Rosien had been born in Lake Champlain, but Pep came from Ireland. They'd just come to the states when they rescued me. Did they swim all the way here? I probably wouldn't know that part of the story for awhile, but from all the things I learned that summer, the one that surprised me the most was just how little you can really know about people, even when you think you know it all.

I'm not just talking about the fact that I never knew, never even guessed, my parents were silkies. Living, breathing fairy tales that tucked me in at night.

But I'm also talking about myself. I never knew, never would have guessed, I'd ever put my foot in water again, let alone learn how to swim.

We'd live like everybody else during the day, then at night Mem and Pep would patrol the lake for wayward boats or foolish swimmers. Me, I'd be home in bed, dreaming of following them in a sailboat with the moon to guide me—at least that's the dream I'd had for three nights running, each time with Tylo jumping and waving at me from the beach, shouting, "Wait for me!"

And now the morning after having that dream a fourth time, I stood on the beach sporting my first-in-a-long-time swimsuit—purple with blue butterflies. Not bad. I walked right into that water so that Mem could give me my first swimming lesson.

She held my head as I leaned back into the water, saying, "You know, in the winter, when the vacationers go home, we can swim silkie pretty much any time we like."

Pep came to swim round us. "And in a good diving suit, you won't feel the cold at all."

As I lay there in the water, my arms fanning out, my back wet, my muscles loose, my parents swimming like a net around me, I believed I could float. Knew I would swim. And for the first time since my mom walked me into the water as a wee child, I couldn't wait.

# ABOUT THE AUTHOR

A long time ago at a beach on the St. Croix River, I stepped into a sinkhole and flailed to get back to the surface. Luckily, my mom saw me go under and came to the rescue. It took me quite awhile to get over my fear of water. And I remember coaching myself to not let the fear win. I love to swim now. So I wanted to give Kyna that kind of victory too. And who am I? I'm Alexandria LaFaye. The author of this book and a handful of others. I used to live on Lake Champlain—but I never did catch sight of a silkie. Now I live in Cabot, Arkansas, and teach in the low residency MFA Programs at Hamline and Hollins universities. Let me know what you think of Kyna's story at www.alafaye.com.

Photo by Rhonda Hunt

# MORE BOOKS FROM
# MILKWEED EDITIONS

To order books or for more information, contact
Milkweed Editions at (800) 520-6455 or visit our
Web site (www.milkweed.org).

*Perfect*
Natasha Friend
Milkweed Prize for Children's Literature

*The Linden Tree*
Ellie Mathews
Milkweed Prize for Children's Literature

*Remember As You Pass Me By*
L. King Pérez

*The Cat*
Jutta Richter
Mildred L. Batchelder Honor Book

*Behind the Bedroom Wall*
Laura E. Williams
Milkweed Prize for Children's Literature
Jane Addams Peace Award Honor Book

# MILKWEED EDITIONS

Founded in 1979, Milkweed Editions is one of the largest independent, nonprofit literary publishers in the United States. Milkweed publishes with the intention of making a humane impact on society, in the belief that good writing can transform the human heart and spirit.

# JOIN US

Milkweed depends on the generosity of foundations and individuals like you, in addition to the sales of its books. In an increasingly consolidated and bottom-line-driven publishing world, your support allows us to select and publish books on the basis of their literary quality and the depth of their message. Please visit our Web site (www.milkweed.org) or contact us at (800) 520-6455 to learn more about our donor program.

Milkweed Editions, a nonprofit publisher, gratefully acknowledges sustaining support from Anonymous; Emilie and Henry Buchwald; the Patrick and Aimee Butler Family Foundation; the Dougherty Family Foundation; the Ecolab Foundation; the General Mills Foundation; the Claire Giannini Fund; John and Joanne Gordon; William and Jeanne Grandy; the Jerome Foundation; Constance and Daniel Kunin; the Lerner Foundation; Sanders and Tasha Marvin; the McKnight Foundation; Mid-Continent Engineering; the Minnesota State Arts Board, through an appropriation by the Minnesota State Legislature, a grant from the Wells Fargo Foundation Minnesota, and a grant from the National Endowment for the Arts; Kelly Morrison and John Willoughby; the National Endowment for the Arts; the Navarre Corporation; Ann and Doug Ness; Ellen Sturgis; the Target Foundation; the James R. Thorpe Foundation; the Travelers Foundation; Moira and John Turner; Joanne and Phil Von Blon; Kathleen and Bill Wanner; and the W. M. Foundation.

MINNESOTA
STATE ARTS BOARD

NATIONAL
ENDOWMENT
FOR THE ARTS
A great nation
deserves great art.

TARGET.

THE McKNIGHT FOUNDATION

Interior design by Steve Foley
Typeset in ITC Giovanni Book
by Steve Foley
Printed on acid-free Glatfelter paper
by Friesens Corporation